The
Terminal Option

The
Terminal Option

John Thomas Rogers

The Storyteller's Collection

Destiny Image Publishers
P.O. Box 310
Shippensburg, PA 17257-0310

ISBN 1-56043-656-5

For Worldwide Distribution
Printed in the U.S.A.

Destiny Image books are available through these fine distributors outside the United States:

Christian Growth, Inc.,
Jalan Kilang-Timor, Singapore 0315

Successful Christian Living
Capetown, Rep. of South Africa

Lifestream
Nottingham, England

Vision Resources
Ponsonby, Auckland, New Zealand

Rhema Ministries Trading
Randburg, South Africa

WA Buchanan Company
Geebung, Queensland, Australia

Salvation Book Centre
Petaling, Jaya, Malaysia

Word Alive
Niverville, Manitoba, Canada

Acknowledgements

I wish to thank Kevin Korb for the time he spent helping me work through the first very rough draft. His ideas were excellent and helped to make this book what it is. There have been several others as well. A special thanks goes to my wife, Beabea, my mom and dad, and our friends, Paul Fay, Penny Toomer, Louise Lyon, Michael Wilkinson, and Rachel James who read early versions and encouraged me with their positive comments.

A special thanks needs to be made to Keith Carroll at Destiny Image, whose cheerful attitude never quits. His continual refusal to give up may well be the reason this book is published.

I also want to thank Cathy Nori for her tough analysis that truly helped to develop the book as well as Cathy Ramey for her excellent reviews and notes. An additional thank you is needed for Paul deParrie whose positive comments and direction were very useful. Finally, a special thank you to Larry Walker for the hours of editorial work that he did on the manuscript. May God bless all of you in your war for life.

Dedication

For Christy

Contents

Foreword

In *The Terminal Option*, John Rogers brings us a disturbing vision of a future where selfishness has become the prime virtue, treachery a plus, and willfulness a mark of superiority. The seeds of today sprout into the terrors of tomorrow.

Rogers needs not to be a prophet in the biblical sense to bring us this new world. The developments of *The Terminal Option* will surprise you—and you will see how easily they might actually come to pass. But this is no hopeless dystopia. In the world of Rogers' future there burns a light—a small but steady beacon of hope.

The Terminal Option will grip you with its all-too-human conflicts as you are propelled into a world without moral walls.

Completely apart from direct Divine intervention, there are consequences to our acts—both as individuals and as a society. One of modern man's problems is that he fails to recognize this and, thus, does not extrapolate into the future considering his future actions—and take heed.

The Terminal Option opens a window of time before us, revealing the fearful terrors of tomorrow. I pray we act before such a future is upon us.

Paul deParrie
August, 1992

Prelude

America

Year 2106
(Historical start of the Canadian Conflict)

Dateline: March 15, 2106

Location: Washington, D.C.

"I have grown tired of hearing about the good ol' days from those people who wish to go back to doing their own laundry, washing their own dishes, fixing their own vehicles, dying of cancer, working forty-hour-a-week jobs with only two weeks of vacation a year, and all of the other harsh realities associated with the primitive twenty-first century.

"I am here to say that we live in the best time of human history! Pollution is no longer an issue, and most of our offspring are only vaguely aware that nuclear war had at one time been a possibility. There is so much about our time that we can rejoice in! The reality of cold fusion warms our homes and fuels our travels. With a beam of light we can travel to any point on our planet and the moon. Soon, we will travel the universe in such a fashion.

"We have health, happiness, enjoy sexual pleasure of any nature without criticism, and are able to develop our own human potential without fear of prejudice. We live in the best period of human achievement. Let us never return to the dark ages of religious dominance and tyranny!"

Sir Alex Tyler
Before the Grand Council

Dateline: June 6, 2106

Location: South Central Canada

"It is good to be with you this day here in the southern woods of your great nation. You are my friends, and we have shared so much together. You have chosen to sacrifice all that modern man believes will make your life valuable—for the very belief that life is valuable in itself. You live in secret, fight evil where no one sees, and die before a world that applauds your death. You are true warriors, and I am honored to be counted among you.

"I have asked you here because soon there will be war between Canada and the United States. Your nation will no longer tolerate the cruelty of mine, and it is time to end the slaughter that occurs each day at the death mills of the Grand Council. You are being called upon to help in this conflict, for the Underground Railroad has many connections with which to aid the Canadian government. Your assistance will be invaluable. I long and pray for the day when I will be proud once again to be an American."

Councilman Jonathan Ames
Organizational Meeting
Strike Force Four

PART I

Beginnings

Year 1996

Chapter One

2:00 a.m.

There was very little light, but there was life. Nothing much filtered through the surrounding walls into her world of soft fluid and cushioned barriers. She had been small at first, very tiny, but that had changed rapidly in the first few months of her existence. Expanding, stretching, enlarging. Searching, questioning, wondering—not by analyzation, but through the channel of emotion. She reached out, feeling. Growing, smiling, yawning—waiting. Uncertain, but secure. Very secure. Warm, protected.

Startled. Pressure, sensing discomfort. Squirmed. Enough of that. The child kicked against her protective womb causing her mother to turn over and wake up. Tasha sat up in bed with a start, staring into the darkness of her room. Alone and afraid, she slid back into the protection of the bed's sheets and pulled the covers up to her cheeks. Relaxing her hand on the blanket, she tried to calm herself, but Tasha was wide awake. She knew that a long night of sleepless gazing into emptiness was ahead of her. She searched the room with weary eyes, but nothing came into her vision. Everything was dark.

6:00 a.m.

Tossing and turning with her hands to her ears, Tasha squeezed her eyelids together so tightly that tears came to her eyes as she tried to blot out the scenes that flashed rapidly through her mind. Against her will—hating every part of the memory, she found herself once again reliving the terrifying experience that did not let her sleep.

Tasha once again stood in front of a huge building complex that looked somewhat like a hospital. Shouting and anger were all around her as a massive crowd pushed against her body, and Tasha was frightened by the hysteria of anarchy that engulfed her. Police sirens screamed in her ears while flashing lights illuminated the scene.

She heard someone cry for help in the middle of the confusion, and she looked to see where the cry came from. She caught brief images of uncontrolled mania through the moving heads and arms about her, as wilding swaying signs partially blocked her view.

In the distance, Tasha caught glimpses of people chained to the entrance of the large women's clinic in front of her. When the crowd parted for a moment, she saw the bizarre sight of several people viciously beating and kicking an elderly nun.

What was she doing here? Tasha thought to herself. The woman at the counseling center had promised her that the abortion could be done without interference, but there was no way to get to the front door of the clinic. She checked her watch as someone shoved against her again.

4

It was past her appointment time. She heard another piercing scream and more excited shouts. Fear overwhelmed her—she knew she had to get away from this insane place!

Tasha opened her eyes, surprised that the memory of the previous day's happenings faded only partially from her mind. She sat up on her bed and curled her legs up to her chin, wrapping her arms around her knees. She watched the light of the room increase slowly as daylight became a part of the early morning. The sunlight caused her to give an involuntary shake as it warmed her chilled body. She kept her eyes hidden in the darkened portion of the room away from the light. Her own soul felt cold—as if she was hardening her heart against the decision that lay before her.

Tasha's morning was already a long one because she had not slept since those early hours when the baby's kicking woke her from a sound sleep. She shook her head. *It's not a baby,* she reminded herself. She was weary from wrestling the demon of despair and guilt inside of her mind. There were moments that it seemed her head would pound itself off of her body.

She felt the contour of her tummy beneath the nightgown. It was clearly showing her pregnancy. The carefully selected dresses would not hide the truth much longer. She let out a discouraged sigh. If she was going to do it, she had very little time to waste before everyone knew her condition.

She wished she could be like Mary, her closest friend, who had been able to terminate her pregnancy without any guilt. "The fetus is just another organ in your body,"

Mary had said. "Removing it is like removing an unwanted growth or cancer."

Tasha shook her head with the memory. She did not feel that what was inside her was a cancer, it was wonderful—even with the morning sickness, she felt a real sense of completeness. Later on in her life, after she had married, it would be the fulfillment of a dream. Now, all it had caused her was pain.

Mary was not being hard-hearted when she got her abortion. At first, she was both excited and somewhat terrified about her conception—she talked a lot about keeping the child. At least she did until her boyfriend, Steve, moved into the picture. Before long, Mary had become totally convinced that her pregnancy was a plague that would ruin her future. Steve had a lot of plans and wanted Mary to share them with him. The issue was settled and the abortion was done. Steve even paid for it. Why couldn't Jeff be like that?

Jeff...his honest smiling face came to Tasha's mind. *He was such an innocent kid in a lot of ways*, she thought. She knew that in her own way, she had set him up. It wasn't difficult to channel his feelings of love into the responses she wanted. At the time, it had seemed pretty romantic manipulating him as she did. Maybe that wasn't fair, but Tasha felt she was being left behind.

Other girls her age were always sharing their experiences with each other. Some of her friends had some pretty wild stories, and all Tasha had was her ignorance. She marveled at how, in just a few short moments, a wrong decision could ruin a person's life. It had seemed so right at the time—why did she have to get pregnant?!

Her parents had fallen apart when she told them. They were not the most religious family, but the relatives were, and "baby" was a major embarrassment to her father. He seemed more concerned about what the relatives would think than about what his own daughter was going through.

Tasha would never forget sitting in that uncomfortable old chair her dad kept in the study, listening to him rant and rave at her for what seemed like hours. He paced back and forth, over and over again, and then he would suddenly stop and viciously turn on her. He would point his finger and start yelling at the top of his lungs. He had acted this way before, but this time he seemed more brutal about it. She remembered his words. They hurt.

"Why?!" he shouted. "Haven't I taken care of you? Haven't I given you a good home?! Bought you a new car?! Given you every chance to make something of yourself?! And you throw it all away just because you want to show everyone how grown up you are!" After a string of curses, he continued, "Well, you're grown up all right, and it won't be long before everyone knows!"

"Daddy, I'm sorry. I don't want to hurt you. Jeff and I..." she tried to share as she began sobbing.

"Don't bring that boy's name up to me!" her father interrupted. "As far as I'm concerned, he just used you. What was he—stupid or something? Didn't he know how to keep you from getting pregnant?"

Tasha found herself going to Jeff's defense. "Dad, he's not that kind of guy. It happened, but it was as much my fault as his. No, actually it's your fault! You drove me to it—always talking about how I didn't fit in—that the other business associates' daughters were more flashy than I was…"

"So now it's my fault?!" he responded in anger. Tasha had thought it wasn't possible for him to get louder, but he did. "I suppose you did this to get even with me, to make me look bad. Well, you succeeded. All the relatives will think I'm raising a piece of trash—that I don't know how to train my naive little daughter on how to protect herself. I hope you're proud of yourself! You have always tried to make me look bad…"

"No, Dad…"

"Don't interrupt me when I'm talking!" he shouted. Tasha wondered if the neighbors could hear him. Her mother stepped into the room to try to quiet him and was patiently waiting for an opportunity to speak.

"Dear?" she said.

He turned, pointed his finger at his wife, and said, "You shut up and get out of here!" In terror, her mother turned and left. Now, Tasha felt very much alone, and tried to shut her father out as he raved about disrespect and went on about Jeff and how she really "knew how to pick them." At least Steve supported Mary by paying for her abortion. "I guess I am going to have to pay for the abortion myself," Tasha's father said, his face tightening with emotion.

"What?" Tasha responded with a start.

Her father paused for a moment, then he spoke in a calmer voice, "You heard me. I'm going to pay for your abortion. In fact, I think I'm going to contact the clinic and drop the cash off today." With that, the issue was settled and he turned and left. Tasha's mother came in and put her right arm around her daughter and drew her up close.

"Don't be too hard on your father, dear," she said. "He has a lot of pride. Forgive him."

"What about me, Mother?" Tasha dropped her face into her mother's bosom…"What about me?"

Mother's reaction to the pregnancy had been different than her father's. At first, she sat on the sofa and cried. She found it very difficult to talk, but even so, she seemed to care about Tasha's feelings. Tasha knew her mother would hate the idea of the abortion, but then she also knew that her mother could not stop her. She had not expected her father to demand it, though—that frightened her.

The sun seemed brighter in the sky as Tasha broke free of her memories. She cursed out loud. The whole thing was such a mess—there was going to be no easy way out.

"What should I do, God?" she whispered. Silence. Tasha turned her head as tears began to flow. She moved her lips silently with the words, *I didn't think you would answer.* It did not matter whether she was really giving God a chance to answer or not—she felt bitterness toward Him. Besides, she wasn't sure if she would like His answer.

The phone in her bedroom rang, the personal line her father had given her on her sixteenth birthday just a few months before. Tasha watched it as it rang over and over. It seemed quite insistent. She reached out and picked up the receiver.

"Hello," she said in a quiet voice.

"Hello, Tasha?" came the reply. "Tasha, is that you?" The voice on the other end was also quiet as if a spell might be broken that was somehow protecting them.

"Jeff?" Tasha replied. "I really don't want to talk. We've been through everything already. I'm too tired to deal with it anymore." There was silence for a moment, and Tasha could sense the anger building inside her.

She did not want to feel that way toward Jeff. She felt it was as much her fault as his, but it was easier to shift every aspect of the responsibility in his direction, especially since he didn't want her to go through with the abortion. She knew that Jeff was searching for the right words to say to her on the other end of the line, but her patience was completely gone.

Tasha suddenly exploded in a display of temper, "What do you want from me? You want me to say I'm not going to the clinic today? You want me to say let's go get married? You want me to tell you that I love you? Or do you want the truth?!" Tasha felt regret swell up in her. She didn't want to unload on Jeff, but she was already in too deep to stop now.

"I want the truth," he said, "always the truth."

Tasha felt anger swell again. "I'll tell you the truth. You got me pregnant and then you turned around and got religious. You don't want me to get an abortion, but you don't seem to mind me walking around in front of the neighbors with a baby—" (*No*, Tasha thought, *don't think of it as a baby*) "—with this thing growing big in my insides for everyone to see. If you had to carry it around in your body, you wouldn't do it either!"

"We were wrong. I was wrong. We both made wrong decisions," said Jeff, his voice shaking with emotion. "That doesn't mean that we have to go on making wrong decisions. I want to do the right thing now. I believe with God's help we can—."

That was all Tasha could handle. Cutting him off, she cursed at Jeff and spoke with barely concealed anger, "Mister, you should have thought of that before making this baby—" (*No*, Tasha kicked herself mentally, *it's not a baby. Why do I keep saying that?*)

"Tasha, I love you," Jeff blurted out as he choked back a sob. "I want to share the responsibility of our actions. I do love you, Tasha. I'll help every way I can."

"I hate you," Tasha lied. She wondered if in a way she was really telling the truth. Then to add to his hurt, she said, "I want you to know that it is not your child—" There she was again, talking as if it was a person.

Jeff seemed stunned. "What do you mean?"

"It's my body, Jeff," she said, feeling her anger rise, "so it's my—ah—my cancer to get rid of—even if you helped to make it!"

"No, Tasha, you're wrong."

"Good-by, Jeff. Like I said earlier, we have nothing to talk about. You're only making it harder on me."

As she started to hang up, she heard Jeff's weakened voice reply, "Don't kill our baby, Tasha."

Shaking her head, she placed the receiver down on the phone cradle and whispered, "It's not a baby."

6:45 a.m.

The cool morning air felt brisk on Officer Thompson's arm as it rested on the patrol car door. He leaned his head out of the window to feel the first few rays of the sun surface over the city skyline sprawled across the horizon, then he slid back in and crouched down slightly in the driver's seat. Reaching over for his hat, he placed it on his forehead to cover his eyes. His body was extremely tense, but he knew he could not allow his young partner to know he was nervous. Rookies had a tendency to spook if they sensed their senior officers were unsure of themselves.

Thompson felt very unsure of himself this morning and he knew that he needed to relax. Pretending to doze for a moment would help keep him calm. Besides, he was sleepy. Working two shifts was just about to do him in, but what was a guy to do? His ex-wife knew the exact day and hour his payroll check was issued, and she had a telephone trigger finger that dialed faster than a computer.

"Didn't get enough sleep last night?" asked the junior officer, Dave Young, who sat next to him. "Honestly, Jim, how much longer do you think you can hold down two jobs without collapsing?"

"About five more minutes," came the muffled reply. Thompson's voice trailed off with another statement that was unintelligible.

Young looked out across the street at the J. P. Myer Clinic sitting quietly in the early light of day. The Myer Clinic was known for its research in genetic development and their state-of-the-art abortion procedures. They had the highest safety record in the nation. They also did more abortions than any other hospital or clinic.

"Sure is quiet," Young whispered to himself. There was no response from Thompson except a slight deepening of relaxed breathing. *Wherever Thompson is*, thought Young, *it's miles from here. Might as well let him rest.* The anti-abortion people would be all over the place soon. They never quit.

The current standoff had been going on for about two months with no letup. They generally were not violent, but yesterday they had gotten slightly out of hand. To make maters worse, one of the policemen assigned to protect the clinic had refused to arrest anyone. The poor guy was suspended. *Joe was a good police officer*, Young thought with disgust. *Why had he made that decision?*

It seemed that with each day the anti-abortion people were becoming more and more militant against the law over this issue of women's rights. Yesterday, just as it had happened each day for weeks, about twenty of them sat down on the front and back steps and refused to move. Some of them even chained themselves to the entrance while others were all over the place causing problems. The pro-choice people went bananas as well and attacked several individuals—even an old nun had gotten herself beat up.

13

It took several squads of police officers to clear them out and move the rest of the crowd off the property. The city was growing tired of housing so many people in the jail. The civic leadership had lost their tolerance and patience and were ready to become brutal toward the anti-abortion people.

Young thought it was strange that people who claimed to respect the law, as these people so often did, would be so willing to break it. He wondered if he would ever feel that strong about anything. Probably not, but here he was, defending a health clinic.

He was bothered by the nagging thought that maybe he wasn't really taking a neutral stand after all. Under orders, he was arresting anti-abortion people and defending a pro-abortion organization. The individuals he was arresting were mostly church-going types who wouldn't even break the speed limit under normal circumstances.

Why were they doing this? The question obsessed him, and he kept asking himself if he was defending the civil rights of the clinic owners or just suppressing the rights of others with the authority of law?

The courtroom judges had been handing down extremely tough sentences on these people for more than two decades—but why? These pro-life demonstrators were receiving two and three year sentences with unbelievable fines.

The "anti-nuke" demonstrators who surrounded the Bellis Nuclear Plant at a rally six months ago blocked military vehicles, chained themselves to government property, and threatened several guards and facility officials with physical harm. A federal district judge let them off with a warning and thirty hours of public service—despite the fact that virtually all of the defendents were seasoned anti-nuke protestors and repeat offenders. That didn't seem fair, but he was a cop, and a cop did his job.

Young grinned to himself. *I wonder if those guys shop for their chains and padlocks at the same places the pro-life people do.*

Young and Thompson were assigned the job of making sure that today was not a repeat of yesterday and that no laws were broken. There were several other police vehicles in the area keeping a low profile to avoid causing a direct confrontation with the protestors. Young thought of himself as a good guy that always knew his duty and did it. Why did he have such mixed feelings about this assignment?

Young was not sure where he stood on the issue personally. His girlfriend had gotten an abortion the year before, and at the time it seemed the most practical thing to do. It still did, but some things had started bothering him recently. He had started having thoughts like, *What would my child have looked like if Sally and I had let him live?* The youthful looking officer smiled when he realized that he thought of the unborn baby as a boy. "I guess all men want a son," he said, half out loud.

"What?" asked the sleeping patrolman. "What did you say?"

"Nothing," replied Young. He thought about the officer dozing in the seat next to him. He was a good senior officer who had a lot of problems with his personal life. *Being a police officer tended to destroy anyone's personal life,* thought Young. One thing about Thompson, he never let his emotions get out of control—despite what he was feeling inside.

Young wondered what Thompson would do if he knew of the plans that several other officers had for the women protestors they knew they would be arresting today. He had overheard a conversation in the locker room the previous night that troubled him. Some of the policemen planned to take advantage of the hand search regulations with any pro-life women taken into custody today.

He was too inexperienced to know what to do in this politically run police department. He should talk it over with Thompson, but that might give the impression that he was a troublemaker, and Young did not want to make waves. *Feeling guilty is not much of a comfort either*, he thought. Any regret he was feeling faded from memory as he watched a packed church bus pull up and began to count the number of pro-life demonstrators climbing out with picket signs.

7:45 a.m.

Tasha felt very much alone as she stood with a small group of women outside the counseling center waiting for the vans to arrive. After failing to get her abortion the day before, Tasha had returned to the center hoping to be given a solution to her problem. They had informed her that the pro-choice people were going to escort women into the Myer Clinic by force, and if she wanted an abortion, she needed to be waiting outside the counseling center by a quarter to eight the next day.

All night long, Tasha had wrestled the issue back and forth trying to decide. Now her mind was beyond thinking, her actions were mechanical. The vans pulled up with smiling attendants and she climbed in.

Chapter Two

8:00 a.m.

Officer Young helped to gently push back the crowd that was pressing toward the sidewalk. *The anti-abortion people seem to be pretty submissive,* he thought. *They haven't done anything out of control yet. Maybe this day will pass quietly enough.*

Some things just don't work out, he thought as he turned his head and noticed several vans pulling up and a large collection of people climbing off. The signs they carried were full of slogans indicating that the pro-choice people had arrived to help safely escort any women wanting to enter the clinic.

Young smiled inwardly. Thompson had told him he had never witnessed an occasion when a pro-lifer injured an abortion clinic client in all the years he'd been defending abortion clinics.

The young officer felt his sixth sense go off—this new group of activists seemed very determined, as if they knew they were there to accomplish a specific task.

19

A militant feeling swept through both groups as the pro-abortion people began to maneuver down the sidewalk to form a wall of men and women on both sides.

Without warning, before Officer Young or the opposing demonstrators could stop them, some pro-life people quickly crawled on hands and knees through the crowd up to the front of the clinic where they quickly chained themselves to the bars that covered the door.

Three television crews had already arrived, evidently to film the arrival of the pro-choice vans. Young had felt uneasy earlier when the TV cameras and reporters arrived a few minutes before. Now he was in a confused daze as to where everyone was coming from.

Before he could act, the television people quickly angled their cameras toward the front entrance. The whole city watched as the anti-abortion people once again successfully blocked the front door of the Myer Clinic.

Realizing what had just taken place, Officer Young made a couple of disgusted comments under his breath as he felt the pressure of the anti-abortion group against him. From around the back of the building, someone shouted, "They've chained themselves to the back door as well!"

Another van of people drove up as Officer Thompson called for backup. A dozen-or-more pregnant women stepped from the van while someone pleaded from somewhere in the surging crowd, "Don't do it! Love your baby!"

An angry voice behind Young yelled, "Shut up! It's her choice!" Then both sides exploded in vocal combat as the noise level became almost unbearable. Young noticed that Thompson, his partner, had appeared beside him, trying to get control of the situation.

"Listen to me!" said someone in the crowd who reached through the wall of people and took hold of the arm of a young pregnant girl. The voice seemed calm enough. "Please, let your child live." The frightened teenager looked into the eyes of the older woman who had taken hold of her, and remembered seeing her at her father's firm. Tasha knew the older lady recognized her as "the boss's daughter," but she could not turn away. There was something about this woman that seemed to communicate that she cared for her.

In the brief moment the two of them shared in that chaotic scene, the middle-aged lady sensed the teen's desperate loneliness. *Poor Tasha*, the lady thought. She wanted to reach out and embrace the teenager. Suddenly, another person's arm came down hard, violently breaking the contact between the two.

"Get away from her!" a man in his twenties shouted. The older woman felt herself shoved back. Television cameramen came running as two more patrol cars pulled up.

Jessica stood upright before the wall of people that had tightened in front of her. She knew that she had broken her group's rules of conduct regarding physical contact when she reached out to the young woman, but she had been so compelled. Now, anger began to build inside of her. She fought to control it.

"Mister," she said, "don't do that again!" The cameras were all around them trying to get shots of the confrontation, but they were not able to get close because people from both groups were pressing inward. Police officers on the outer edge were trying to get to the site of the confrontation at the same time.

In the middle of the confusion, Jessica felt someone violently kick her shins. Instantly—out of pure reflex—she pushed back in defense in the direction of the person causing the pain. She saw the cameras zero in on her and suddenly realized they could only see her pushing—not the person kicking her. Jessica tried to pull back, but it was too late. As the pushing and shoving accelerated into an open melee, she knew she would be labeled the instigator. Everything was out of control.

9:20 a.m.

Tasha's mother was curled up on the living room sofa watching the news report when her daughter came through the front door. The newswoman reported that a riot started by the anti-abortion people had broken out at the Myer Clinic. There seemed to be several injuries.

"Tasha," her mother said, "I was worried about you going down to the clinic today. I was afraid it would be very dangerous."

"I'm all right, Mother," Tasha responded, "I've made up my mind. I'm not going through with the abortion!"

The older woman looked up for a moment from the television set. "Dear, do you think that your father will accept that?"

"No," Tasha replied. "I think he will blowup!" She watched as her mother stood up, with concern etched on her face. The older lady walked over to her daughter and placed her arm around Tasha's shoulder in her usual manner.

"I don't want you hurt," her mother shared.

Traces of anger crossed Tasha's face and then traveled inward. *How dare she claim to care!* she thought. Memories of the long days of aching loneliness from her childhood with no parent being present flashed back in her mind. She shoved her mother's consoling arm off her shoulder and snapped, "Forget it, Mom! Don't give me that! It's too late for it."

Tasha turned away as she started to shake, her emotions swirling like a whirlwind inside of her. She wanted the swirling to stop, but none of the feelings would settle. She could not get control and found herself blurting out, "You never stood up for me in front of Dad!

"I went to get the abortion early this morning because I didn't know what else to do. I was walking in to get it done when a woman stopped me and asked me to let my child live. It was Jessica, Mother. Dad's going to be so angry at her—he'll probably fire her, but I couldn't go on with it. I got away from the crowd and talked to several ladies by the church bus who told me abortion would be the wrong thing to do. They made sense, Mother. God does not want us to take human life—any life—no matter how small!"

Tasha paused a moment, then said, "They also talked about Jesus Christ. I don't know what I'm going to do about that yet. I've still got to think about it."

The mother reached out her hand to her daughter. She spoke softly. "Religion has its place, but God won't get you out of this!"

Tasha responded instantly, "I don't want to be a murderer and kill my own child!"

"You're not a murderer!" the mother fired back. "I don't want you to have to get an abortion if you don't want to!"

"Tell that to my father!"

"I've tried," the older lady responded. "He won't listen to me. I'm afraid he might make you get the abortion anyway. He is set on you getting it—I don't believe either of us can change his mind. Perhaps you should go back to the clinic before your father comes home."

Tasha started to curse but caught herself. Instead she said, "Mother, it's my life, my insides, my hurt and my problem—what does Dad have to do with this?! He's never been pregnant. He's always telling me how to live!"

Tasha's mother took her by the shoulders with her hands and looked straight into her eyes. "Honey, God does not want you to live a miserable life with an unwanted child. That would be cruel to the child as well. I think you ought to go back and terminate the pregnancy!"

"When did you start to worry about what God thinks?" Now Tasha was really mad at her mom for acting so spiritual. "You haven't been to church since I was a little girl. Why don't you leave me alone!" Her mother reached out to her again, but Tasha pulled away and stepped back. "Just leave me alone!"

Fear—even terror—suddenly gripped the older woman. Bitter tears broke from the corners of her eyes as her face seemed to age right before Tasha's eyes, and then the daughter saw the rage—it was deep and bitter.

"Are you crazy, Tasha!" her mother cried. "Your father will beat us both when he comes in!" The mother caught herself before the full force of her anger broke free from its well-disciplined prison. She calmed herself and spoke softly to her daughter, "Honey, your father and I love each other, but he is under a lot of stress. You need to be more patient with us."

"I know the story, Mother." Inside, Tasha was starting to weaken. Oh God, she thought, if I listen to my mom, she'll talk me into going back to the clinic. "Mother," she said firmly, "I love you, but I can't deal with this any longer. Can't you see that? I'm going to go crazy." Her mother reached over to put her arm around Tasha again. This time, the young woman did not push her mother away. Instead, she folded inward to the touch and allowed her mother's strength to sustain her.

"Tasha," her mother spoke softly, "give yourself time to enjoy life. Don't spend your early years taking care of a family. You ought to be free having a good time!

I'll go with you to the clinic if that would help?" Tasha pushed her mother away hard.

"Oh, Mother," she said, shaking her head, "you don't understand." She paused a moment. "I don't think you want me to solve this! Are you more concerned with what people think than you are about me? Are you concerned about me? Mother, are you concerned about me?"

Her mother turned away.

"I didn't think so." Tasha continued. "God in heaven, I'm trapped!"

Her mother spoke, almost ashamed, "If you don't love Jeff, there are other boys. Do you think they'll want you now—with a brat hanging onto your jeans? They'll figure you're good for one thing, and the kid will prove it to them!"

"Don't talk like that," Tasha pleaded.

"You're better than that." Her mother responded. "We should have put you on the pill like that counselor suggested, but you told me you were a virgin."

Tasha felt frustration rising inside her. She felt her will weakening. With growing weariness, she answered, "I was, Mother. Jeff is the only boy I've ever been with, and I've only done it one time. I wish to God that I hadn't, but it's done and I want to put it behind me." As her mother turned to her, Tasha sighed deeply and continued, "Maybe you are right. If you feel this is the answer, then I will go back to the clinic."

Tasha sensed a horrible sadness overwhelm her. She felt for a moment that she was about to pass out. Now there was nothing left to be said—there was no reason not to go ahead. She felt empty as she walked toward the front door.

Tasha paused at the door and faced her mother, who seemed unable to look her in the face.

"Mother?"

"Yes?"

"If you had been where I am when you were my age and found yourself pregnant with me, would you have done to me what I am about to do..." Tasha paused and then continued, "...to my child?"

Her mother answered in a cold, controlled voice, "Honey, I did do it—with your older sister."

Startled, Tasha said, "I don't have an older sis-...." Horror swept over her.

"I'm sorry, Tasha," her mother offered. "I was going to tell you about the abortion, but I was too ashamed."

Tasha recovered herself quickly. "Forget it, Mother. There is nothing to be ashamed of." She turned and went out the door. Tasha's feelings of softness toward the life inside her was rapidly leaving her emotions. In its place was a cold hardness that could see only the stony ridges of her father's face.

Standing alone in the silent room, Tasha's mother spoke softly. "Yes, there is shame, years of shame." Then, after a weary shake of her head, she walked out the front door to join her daughter.

9:45 a.m.

Officer Young carefully scanned the scene in front of the clinic. He was beginning to think that maybe the crowd was starting to settle down. They had managed to arrest the protestors that had chained themselves to the clinic's doors. The prisoners were already enroute to the police station. The news people were setting up an interview with a spokesman from each side of this controversy that seemed to be holding everyone's attention.

Young considered the situation. *We might yet live through this day.* The policeman felt the edge of a terrible headache forming around his forehead. He was not in the mood for any more trouble.

10:15 a.m.

Jeff brought his car to a stop about a block from the Myer Clinic. It was as close as he could get with all the television vehicles and police cars. As he sat there, his mind went back to pretty Tasha and the first moment they had met a couple of years before. He had been out jogging when he topped a hill and saw her right in front of him, wearing fashion jeans and bent over a twisted-up bicycle. When she stood up and looked at him, he saw a bruise on her forehead and a trickle of blood running from a scratch on her arm.

"Are you all right?" he had asked.

She looked at him in disgust and replied, "Of course I am. This is my repair shop…" She pointed to the empty landscape surrounding them. "…and I'm very busy with this customer's bicycle, so state your business and move on!"

"Sorry," Jeff said somewhat sheepishly. "You've had a wreck."

"Sharp guy," Tasha responded. "Don't you just hate being right all the time?"

"No, but I've learned to live with it," Jeff replied with a grin. He walked over and picked up the broken bicycle. "Here, I'll carry this for you. Where do you live?"

It was Tasha's turn to smile. "Oh, about six miles from here," she said.

Jeff paused to give her a pained look, then responded, "OK, lead on." Actually, Tasha lived less than a mile away. Jeff shook his head with the memory. She was always teasing him. He loved her so much.

As he made his way to the edge of the large crowd surrounding the front entrance of the abortion clinic, he wondered if Tasha had already come. *Life is hard,* he thought. *I wish I had made better decisions. God, reach Tasha. Don't let her do this thing, this awful thing.*

Jeff stood and watched the crowd for a moment, reading the signs carried by the different groups. He could not blame Tasha. He understood some of the shame as well as the desire to somehow remove the guilt and the weight of responsibility.

He walked across the street and entered the crowd of pro-lifers. Some of them knew him and waved. He waved back as he moved toward the TV cameras. An interview had already started, and he wanted to hear what was being said. As he moved closer, he heard a female news reporter speaking to an older woman representing the pro-life side.

"What is wrong with a woman having control of what happens with her body?" the reporter asked.

Jessica spoke calmly, even though she felt anger at the question. "The child inside is not her body. It is a real human being. The fact that it is attached to its mother is no different than a patient attached to a life-sustaining machine. The patient is not a part of the machine, he or she is only being sustained by it until the patient is able to leave the hospital.

"The unborn baby is not a disposable body part of the mother, he or she is an independent living person who is being sustained by the mother until it is time to leave the womb at birth. The mother will continue to sustain the baby after birth by nursing it. That is how God meant it to be."

Leaning closer toward the cameras, Jessica continued, "Having a living person inside you doesn't give you the right to do with it—or to *DO AWAY WITH IT*—as you please. Bringing life into this world is a privilege God gives to mothers. It is wrong to abuse it."

"How can you claim that a piece of tissue growing inside a person is individual life?" interjected the pro-choice spokeswoman. "The issue is quality life. The fetus has no quality of life until it is exposed to the world and begins to learn."

Jessica quickly replied, "Where is the line of *quality* life for you? Is it when a child nurses, walks for the first time, or successfully learns the multiplication tables? How can you say that life isn't *quality* until it meets your standards?

"There was a time when the Jews in Germany and the blacks in our nation were not considered *quality* life. It was that kind of thinking that *justified* their enslavement, torture and wholesale murder by their countrymen!" As the cameras and the crowd focused in, Jessica shared her heart, "Our nation has decided that unborn children are not people—despite the fact that they have their own genetic code, permanent fingerprints, and God's blessing-."

The pro-choice woman started trying to interrupt, but Jessica would not stop. "…we as a people have decided they are non-human for no other reason than that we want to have our pleasure—free of responsibility! We are in danger of God's judgment as a people. I'm afraid God will just allow us to live with our choices—wherever they may lead us—because surely we deserve their final consequences."

This was all the pro-choice representative could stand. Her response was angry and uncontrolled. "Shut up, you religious bigot! What do you understand of freedom and responsibility?! How dare you put a guilt trip like that on us! We have constitutional rights. You anti-choice women are against everything." She started to make another statement when Jessica interrupted.

"Everyone should have freedom of choice, but not to kill! A woman makes her choice when a baby is conceived. I'm here to stand against the slaughter of innocent children in that building!" Jessica said, pointing toward the abortion clinic. "I am pro-life, not anti-life! We must face the truth! Pro-choice is just another term for pro-death!"

With Jessica's last statement, the crowd on both sides exploded in a crescendo of angry shouts and accusations, and the police started moving in.

In the middle of the pushing and shoving, Jeff caught a glimpse of Tasha walking toward the clinic's entrance with her mother.

Desperation swept through him. Almost at the point of panic, Jeff knew he had to find a way to stop her before she allowed them to take his child's life.

Forcing his way through the crowd, he shouted, "Tasha! Wait a minute! I want to talk to you!" Tasha saw him and started running toward the front door of the clinic. The "rescuers" who had chained themselves to the entrance had already been removed. Jeff desperately tried to get in front of her to stop her.

Several people in the pro-choice crowd saw what was happening and quickly jumped on Jeff to hold him down. As they struggled with him, Jeff felt rage at their interference. Breaking one arm free, he slugged a man full in the face with his fist and threw a woman to the ground. "Let go of me!" he screamed. More of them surged toward him, and the police were there.

Officer Young put handcuffs on Jeff as Thompson pulled the angry crowd off of him. "Calm down, buddy," Young said sternly. "We gotta get you out of here in one piece."

Jeff looked frantically for Tasha. She was standing by the entrance with the door half open. "Don't," he shouted at her above the confusion. "Please, don't!" After wiping tears from her eyes, Tasha slowly turned away from him and walked into the building. As the door closed behind her, Jeff felt hot tears flowing down his cheek.

"Pull yourself together," Officer Thompson said as he helped his partner lift Jeff to his feet.

"You don't understand," Jeff said with a semi-controlled sob. "She is going to let them kill my baby."

"I understand," said Officer Young and moved Jeff toward the patrol car.

11:00 a.m.

Fear, uncertainty. Sensing stress and emotion from outside the womb. Voices talking—familiar, not so familiar. The child stretched and moved, forcing her mother to take note of her. There was still warmth. There was still security. The child relaxed. Now she felt somewhat different, almost druggish. *Pressure.* She pulled back. *More pressure. Pain.* Recoiling to safety against the wall of the womb—next to the place of love and protection, peace and security. *Trust. Pain again. No where to move. Pain.* She reached out to push away. *Desperate. Pain. Her hand—it was pulling away from her arm. More pain. Scream—no sound. Pulling, tearing.*

Terror.

Panic.

Jerking.

Pain.

Death.

PART II

Dignity

Year 2052
(56 years later)

Chapter Three

Valerie stood quietly for a moment outside the towering pillars of the Church of Remembrance. The beautiful cathedral dated back into the early twentieth century and had a long history of New Age involvement. That pleased Valerie immensely—she felt strong life force impressions as she stood in this place. The building had fallen into partial collapse with the 2018 earthquake and the structure was weakened considerably. Restoration had been a tricky process, but judging from the appearance, it was quite successful.

Valerie always enjoyed analyzing the old church since she relished any object from the past. She mused further as she walked up the majestic stairway to the large heavy doors that guarded the inside of the building and the history of the people it protected. The doors automatically opened for her as she approached. Walking through them, she caught a glimpse of the Aztec writings that covered the portals above her. She had been told that it was an ancient burial chant which spoke of joining oneself with the earth and sky. Valerie sensed a great calmness as she entered the doorway. Her heart was at home here.

Someone made a movement in front of her—the spell was broken. It was just a visitor leaving the building, but it was enough to bring Valerie back to the reason for her visit. She walked briskly through the wide archway to the front desk in the foyer. An attendant in a very conservative suit watched her approach.

"May I help you, Madam?" he inquired.

"Yes," Valerie replied. "I wish to visit my father." The man activated two controls behind the counter and a screen mounted flush with the counter lit up. Without hesitation, she placed her hand on the glowing screen and an audible tone confirmed positive I.D.

"You may go ahead," the man said and went back to his work. Valerie turned and walked down a long open hallway that she considered very beautiful with its gothic gray appearance. Gray was not her favorite color, but the design was well done. Flowers and plants in basins were built into the structural design of the walls in a very pleasant manner. The feeling was not dismal but of calm sleep.

The next hallway she entered was a mosaic of nature implanted on the walls. The plants of this hallway left the impression of being from the mountains. There was a freshness about this area of the building that she always enjoyed. That was why she had picked this particular hallway for her father's memory.

Valerie stopped by an archway door and placed her hand on a square mounted in the wall at about shoulder height. The square lit up, and the door slid open without a sound. She stepped inside as the door quietly closed behind her. The room was filled with flowers and objects that brought back fond memories of her father. She picked up one of the mementos and placed it gently against her cheek. She released a sad sigh. She missed him.

Walking to the other side of the room, Valerie noticed a new arrangement of flowers. Glancing at the display, she guessed that her brother, Eric, had sent them. They were definitely his style, with their western mountain vase. She shrugged and walked over to the main viewing chairs.

There were six of them, she noted again with a smile. The chairs were very plush and comfortable—not like the cheaper models the funeral director wanted to offer her at a bargain. Valerie remembered how insulted she had felt at the time. Nothing was too good for her daddy.

Valerie sat down and activated the recessed control panel next to the seat. A portion of the wall moved upward out of sight, revealing a fairly large open area. The appearance was dark, like looking into a large cavern, although she could still see the far wall in the dim light. After a moment of silence, music began to play softly.

Still-life pictures began to fade in and out, interspersed and mixed with comments from relatives and occasionally the voice of her father. The still-life pictures began to change and intermix with two dimensional movies both silent and later, with audio.

Valerie found herself relaxing as the story of her father's life unfolded. She felt a sense of pride as she remembered how much she had put into gathering all of the snapshots, films, videos, and tape recordings for this presentation. The funeral home had done an excellent job with her father's memorial. She felt he was so close. Her high priestess had shared with her that the objects kept in the room would draw his spirit there.

Valerie knew that her father's body wasn't really near—the Reanimation Center had no doubt shipped it immediately to the processing plant. She felt a little queasy over what they must have done with his body, but it passed quickly enough. The processing plants were logical. Other living human beings needed what her father's body offered, and it was selfish to not share it. Anyway, she did not have a choice because the government had strict laws concerning recycling.

Settling back in her cushioned viewing chair, she smiled as she thought, *A well-done memorial does so much to comfort the living relatives. It was worth every dollar.*

The story continued unfolding as Valerie sat alone in the viewing room, watching her father and mother teach her how to skip rope. She laughed again as she watched her dad showing off. He was really very good.

There was a blurring sound for a moment and the picture did not flow quite as smoothly as it should have. After a second or two, everything was restored to normal, but Valerie was enraged! *This memorial had been guaranteed against just such failures!* She would complain at the front desk immediately upon completing the viewing.

Now Valerie saw herself at age fourteen. *I was pretty!* she thought. The scene showed her father wrestling with her. She felt uncomfortable for a moment as long-buried memories of some of her father's other actions flashed back to her. She shook her head and continued watching the scene before her.

Valerie noted that she was starting to gain weight in the picture. She had known that she was pregnant at the time, but hadn't settled the issue of whether or not she should get an abortion. Her father had been very open-minded and said the decision was up to her because, after all, it was her body.

Valerie did not want the child. She was afraid it would tie her down, but she could not shake the guilt of the procedure to remove it in its fetal stage. Her mother suggested that she see Master Minh at the Temple.

Valerie rarely visited the Master, so she had entered the automated doors of the modern but oriental-appearing building with a certain level of fear. She was expected.

Her mother had made the appointment earlier, and a young man efficiently ushered her into a beautiful Asian-style office. Sitting in the comfortable surroundings, Valerie's hands slowly released their grip on her chair. She was starting to relax. *Maybe this won't be so bad*, she thought as the Master walked in. She stood up to meet him.

"It is so good to see you again, Valerie," the older man shared. "Your mother has spoken many fine words concerning you. She is very proud."

"Thank you, Master Minh," Valerie responded as she shook his extended hand. He held her hand very warmly for a moment and then released it.

Master Minh turned and very casually sat down in a plush chair next to where Valerie had been sitting. He motioned for her to do likewise. "Young lady, your mother has told me of your pregnancy and your fears of the needed abortion. Why are you afraid?"

Valerie swallowed with a slight amount of difficulty and began speaking. "I'm not certain the abortion is needed. I mean I don't want the child, but–"

"An unwanted child is a terrible thing, Valerie," the Master spoke with authority. "It is very tragic what happens to such children."

"I know that, Master Minh, but I don't want to cause pain to it. Some people say they can feel. I wouldn't hurt a goldfish if I could help it."

Master Minh nodded and spoke soothingly. "I understand, for all life is precious. It is part of a wondrous cycle, ever journeying upward. You and I are part of that cycle. We have traveled, and yet continue to travel that path as well. There is no right or wrong about it. There is no good or evil. The journey is simply that—a journey.

"We choose for our lives what must be done to free ourselves along the way. Often others have chosen pathways that interfere with us. If we possess the power to prevent them, there is no wrong in using that power."

Valerie seemed confused. "Are you saying that this fetus has chosen to interfere with my life?" she asked.

"The entire universe moves by pattern," he responded, "and our life forces are interacting with it. As each life passes, we choose our next journey. You have chosen yours. The fetus has chosen its path as well. Just as you once chose lower forms and experienced the consequences, so must this fetus experience change when it interferes with another more powerful life force."

Valerie was silent for a moment as she analyzed what was being shared with her. Finally she spoke. "Even if what you say is true..."

"It is true."

"Even so," Valerie continued, "I could not take another life force and kill it."

Master Minh nodded in understanding. "Of course— if you were actually killing it—but such an action is an impossibility. On the conscious level of the spiritual plane, there is much more awareness than you realize. The life force tests the body it is considering to dwell in many times during the embryonic stages. It will know when the abortion is about to proceed and immediately depart in search of another body. The doctor will be removing what is only a functioning piece of flesh."

"Then I will cause no pain?" Valerie asked. She was starting to sense relief from the upcoming guilt.

"There is nothing there to feel pain," Master Minh patiently explained. "The fetus recoils during the abortion procedure because of its developing nervous system, not because a living being is in it. My child, go and free yourself of this unwanted life force. It will find another who wants it, and truly it will be much happier."

Master Minh faded from view in Valerie's thoughts as she watched her brother, Eric, playing ball with her dad

43

on the view screen. Her mind quickly went to her phone call with Eric the night before. At first, it was rather unpleasant.

Valerie had been in her room gathering photos of her mother when her house computer announced an incoming phone call. She ignored it, but the synthesizer continued to beep softly. She was not interested in talking to anyone, but her M.A.I.D. 1000 had seemed very insistent that she answer.

She gave in and activated the receiver with an audible command. A middle-aged man appeared before her in three-dimensional form, about a foot beyond her desk at about the height that a man would be if sitting. In fact, she was certain that the man was sitting because she saw the faded impression of a recliner behind him.

"Hello," spoke her quiet voice.

"Hello, Valerie?" came the reply over the receiver. "Valerie, is that you? Activate your video so I can see you. We need to talk."

"Eric," Valerie replied as she completed the instrument command so Eric could see her. "I really don't want to talk. I'm very busy right now. Call me next week."

She was debating whether or not she should tell her brother the plans for the upcoming termination of their mother. She wasn't sure how he would react, and she didn't feel like listening to his criticism. However, enough was enough! She summoned up her courage and spoke. "I'm putting Mother to rest!" she told him.

Eric was silent. Valerie felt impatient as depression swept over her. She did not want to be bitter at Eric. She felt it was as much her fault as his. He was still silent as she thought through her feelings. She knew he was watching and analyzing her.

Valerie knew she hated her brother for acting superior. Unable to endure the quiet between them, she suddenly demanded, "What do you want from me? Do you want me to say that I'm willing to take care of the ol' lady for another twenty years?"

"You are better able to do it than I am," Eric responded. "You get along with her better than I do."

Valerie felt she was beginning to get control of her feelings. "I'll tell you what the real truth is," she interrupted. "You didn't want the responsibility, so you shifted it to me. She belongs to you just as much as she belongs to me!"

Eric's image wavered slightly then came back sharp as he spoke softly, "You didn't tell me you were going to do this!" After a pause, he spoke again, but this time much more harshly. "You said you wanted her! I was trusting you to handle it!"

That was all Valerie could handle. She cursed at Eric and spoke with muffled rage, "Brother, you should have thought of your responsibilities before pulling out!"

"Valerie, I know it's hard," Eric said, choking back his own anger. "I'll help every way I can. I just can't take her back right now."

"I want you to know that I am going to do the termination today!" Valerie answered.

Eric seemed stunned. "No, you can't!"

"Eric," she responded, "are you sure that the reason you don't want to lay mother to rest just yet is because it would give me equal ownership in your company when the will is videoed?"

There was silence in the room as Eric's image hovering above the floor made no sound. Valerie knew she had him and pressed her attack.

"Eric?" There was no response, but she watched a different kind of emotion forming in him. His eyes reflected real hatred, and she knew she would have to cool that before she lost her advantage in the conversation. However, she was starting to enjoy the situation and didn't want to stop her fun right away. "Eric, I know that you have just about convinced Mother to sign over her portion of the company to you."

Eric's eyes had dropped, but now they lifted instantly. "She told you that?" he asked.

"Yes."

"I would have shared the profits with you," he stated.

"Of course you would have!" Valerie nodded in agreement. "That is why you went behind my back and started working this deal, so you could share the profits!"

Eric made no attempt to defend himself. He was convinced that any response he could make would just play into her hands.

"Good-by, Eric," Valerie stated firmly. "Like I said earlier, call me next week. We have nothing to talk about today. You're only making it harder on me." As she started to hang up, she saw the hurt overwhelm Eric's face. Valerie started to push the disconnect button as she heard Eric's weakened voice reply.

"Valerie, don't hang up. Maybe we should talk over my business together. You've always had good ideas and a capable business mind."

That's much better, thought Valerie. "Sure, Eric. I was thinking about flying out next week and sharing a few of my good ideas at your company board meeting. That is a week from Thursday, isn't it?"

"Yes, it is," Eric replied. "Valerie, there is no use for the two of us to fight over our mother like this. I think I probably over-reacted. It's easy to get selfish with a business that you have worked hard at all your life. However, you have almost always been fair with me. Go ahead with the termination. It will be somewhat of a relief for us all."

Valerie found herself softening a little toward her younger brother. She had won the battle and did not feel a need to overdo the victory. "That's all right, Eric. I forgive you. Actually, I am kind of looking forward to working with you. We had a lot of fun growing up together and goofing off. We can do some of that again!"

"I'd like that," Eric nodded with a smile. A strange expression came over his face. "Mother wasn't fair with our dad," he stated.

"I know."

Eric's face tightened. He continued. "I don't know if she ever really loved him. They didn't get along very well. We might as well put her out of her misery like she did him."

Valerie was somewhat shocked at Eric's bluntness, but basically she felt the same way he did. Both of their parents had been pretty selfish, although their dad had been the most likable with his outdoor, easy-going philosophy of life. Valerie would have liked him a lot more if it wasn't for certain things that he had done.

"I agree," Valerie shared. "I'll talk to you later."

"Good-by."

"Good-by, Eric." His image faded from view when she pushed the disconnect button.

With a jolt, Valerie was brought back to the memorial presentation that was unfolding before her. It was her father's laugh that had caught her attention. It ended with that awful cough that he had developed during the last few years of his life. Valerie felt bitterness form in her. It had been that cough that had led to her father's mandatory termination, and her mother had signed the paper work.

The program had switched to mostly three-dimensional videos now with full quality sound. They were the most enjoyable—unfortunately, there were not very many of them. Valerie felt her usual disgust at having failed to take more 3D's of her father. A smile came to her lips as she noted mentally that she had done a much better job with her mother.

Just last week she had picked her mom up and taken her to the environmental park where she had filmed her only remaining parent as she laughed and fed the water-fowl. That had been very satisfying. Valerie turned in the last of her mother's 3D's to the funeral home the day after that outing. Now all the arrangements were made and complete. Valerie felt proud of how she had managed things without her brother's help.

8:26 a.m.

Karl Harrison had been up for several hours and was very proud of himself. For three months he had maintained his new physical fitness schedule despite the hectic daily requirements that always rested on a doctor's shoulders. At thirty-three, he found himself losing some of the enthusiasm for life he had always shown and had decided it was time to change. Today he had jogged four miles and worked out at the spa. It was great!

After jumping in and out of the shower, he dressed quickly, thinking about the busy day that lay ahead of him. Karl really did not mind being busy because he was not a lazy man. He smiled. One does not become the head administrator of a Reanimation Center at thirty-three by sleeping in and partying. The thought brought another smile to Karl's lips. Tonight was the annual gay activist banquet, and he was the guest of honor. There would be a large number of celebrities there as well as many important governmental officials.

Karl did not practice that particular life style, although he had been involved in one incident in college. However, it was important for his future political career that he be viewed as an open-minded individual who supported the freedom of sexual choice.

His last thought suddenly reminded him of an important detail still left to attend to...CaTai—and her special surprise. It had been two years in the making and now he was ready to make his point in a way she couldn't ignore...

Karl Harrison left his single suite and walked casually down to the elevator. Stepping inside, he pushed the level one button. There was no door closing and no sound as a light came on. He disappeared. Harrison sensed no passage of time as the scene in front of him changed from the hallway to the main lobby. He walked out to the parking terminal where his Starlight - 4 waited on a cushion of air eight inches above the surface. Climbing in, he headed out into traffic.

As he weaved in and out of traffic with a calculated disregard for speed or buffer zone regulations, Karl's thoughts ranged to the first time he and CaTai met at the Global Population Symposium in Zurich two years before.

She had approached him after his masterful speech to the international delegates. She raved about his position on the necessity for bold new steps to control and shape the global destiny through the emerging scientific techniques of advanced genetic cloning, selectivity and modern viability tests.

CaTai was stunningly beautiful, and her position as ranking diplomat on the Social Committee of the European Council implied an impressive intelligence and admirable hunger for power. After an hour of intense political and social exchange, the two found they were compatible in more ways than they cared to admit.

They became the rage of the symposium, and their outrageous escapades in the pleasure domes of the Old German Quarter were the hottest topic of gossip among the Who's Who of Zurich for several weeks.

There was, however, one unfortunate incident that could have complicated both of their careers. Karl grimaced at the thought of his total loss of control that night—he'd nearly killed a child dancer in a brutal beating triggered by the dancer's flirtation with CaTai. He hated himself for his inability to handle RecDrug and E/I (inhanced inebriation) Vodka Chasers, the current rage on the continental party scene.

It was most fortunate the news media supported the symposium's political position and successfully covered up the incident.

Karl comforted himself with the conclusion that he would never have allowed himself to be so careless if Vice Chairman Hendricks from Canada had not taken a sudden opposite opinion to him during one of the panel discussions at the symposium.

On top of everything else, CaTai popped an unexpected surprise: her daily bioscan had picked it up almost immediately.

At first, CaTai's announcement of her unexpected pregnancy was a nuisance to both of them—CaTai was a career diplomat and global politician with a burning hunger for success and power. Karl was every bit her match and more—he'd managed to turn his quick intelligence, good looks and a peculiar disregard for limits or personal morals into a formidable weapon that made him ruthlessly successful in business and politics—he was known to be a dangerous (and deadly) adversary best left alone.

Karl offered to handle the problem quickly at his Reanimation Center in America—after all, it was something he did well—very well. Only minutes before CaTai arrived for the fetal termination, a brilliant plan began formulating in his mind…what better way to demonstrate the value of his program proposal to CaTai than to personally help her solve her problem with the anti-termination people in the European Council?

As usual, Karl executed his plan with deft skill and total secrecy. He decided to handle CaTai's abortion personally to maintain security. Besides, he couldn't resist showing off his own mastery of the unsurpassed American medical termination techniques. Moments after the procedure, Karl produced a quartz lab cube containing the living fetus right before CaTai's shocked face.

"This is your answer to your problems in Europe and the Orient, CaTai!!" he said in hushed tones. "There is one thing EVERYBODY listens to in this world—*cash credits.*"

"Money? What does an aborted fetus have to do with money?" CaTai asked as she reapplied her lipstick.

"You're using it now, CaTai!" Karl said excitedly. "Recycling—the ultimate use and reuse of all biological resources for the good of society and the benefit of humanity—especially *my benefit.* Don't you see it? You bought that lipstick here in America, where the best cosmetics and skin products are made—using *reprocessed human body products!*"

Watching CaTai's lovely eyebrows furrow is disbelief, Karl pressed his case. "Listen CaTai, with your father's business and capital connections and your continental power base in the European Council, I can make us rich and help you solve your little problem with the anti-freedom extremists over there—simply by helping them see that there's money to be made by being realistic and progressive. "It worked in the United States last century…", Karl continued. "It's one of the few true success stories of that period. It's the only known instance where an American industry created and subsidized by the primitive United States government spawned an entire industry unmatched in profitability and unending public demand!"

"I don't know, Karl. Those people in the EC aren't Americans, they're independent representatives of jealous power bases—they don't want anybody to be any richer than they are. And then there is the religious fanatic minority that doesn't seem to understand the importance of human rights or money!" CaTai said as she paused at the entrance to his office. "You'll have to prove it'll work and make it profitable to me before I'm willing to risk my career on the idea."

Karl Harrison had watched her leave and then looked closely at the squirming figure in the 1-liter lab cube he held. Smiling smugly, he thought, *I was hoping you would say that…*

Chapter Four

9:05 a.m.

Old and wrinkled, Tasha leaned forward in her chair and looked toward the lobby of the Manor Retirement Center. Her elderly face twisted in disgust as she glanced at her watch. *Valerie was always slow when you wanted her to hurry, even when she was a child*, she thought.

Her daughter had promised her that she would come by to take her for another outing. *Granted, it isn't natural for Valerie to want to spend so much time with me*, the old woman thought, but she looked forward to every occasion to get out.

Time at the Retirement Center weighed heavily on Tasha even though the staff made some attempts to create diversion. None of the things they offered appealed to her.

She laughed at herself, but it was not a laughter of happiness, only a dismal laughter of failure. All her great plans for joy in life had come to nothing. Her manipulation of people had always led to disaster. She had plenty of money, but what was that when there was no one there to share life with. Most of her time was spent dwelling on the past, leaving her even more depressed.

Until recently, no one had bothered to visit her at all. Then quite suddenly, Valerie had begun to spend more and more time with her. *Eric? He only called to talk about the business*, she thought to herself. She was afraid even that would stop when she signed her share of the business over to him, but then she was afraid he would stop if she didn't.

Memories. Most of the time they are a comfort, Tasha mused. Like yesterday when she was going through her old photographs. She had found one of Jeff, her first real boyfriend. He was so young and innocent looking. That was what she had liked about him. His patience also. You could treat him like dirt, and he still loved you. *I wonder if he is still alive?* Tasha mused inwardly. *I don't even know how to find out.*

After the abortion, Jeff tried several times to contact her, but she had refused. How stupid she had been! Finally, he just quit trying and she had never heard from him since. There was a rumor that he had moved to Canada, but she never was able to find out if it was true.

Canada, she thought. *There were certainly a lot of people moving to Canada in the last few years.* They were pretty much religious fanatics opposing abortion and other fringe social issues. They wanted the freedom to educate their children outside of the state school system. Tasha had once considered religion, but not now. It was too late.

What was I thinking about? she asked herself. *Oh, yes, now I remember. Jeff. He went to Canada or so they said.*

Then Steve came along, full of fun and adventure, with no worry about responsibility. He'd dropped Mary when she became pregnant the second time and started paying attention to Tasha.

Tasha did not want to hurt Mary, but Steve was what she felt she needed right then to forget the hurt. They sure had a wild time together.

In the end, Tasha had become pregnant again too. She refused to get an abortion because of the guilt she had felt over the first one. For some strange reason, Steve felt sorry for her and they got married. Everything went downhill from there.

Valerie was born. Tasha paused in her thoughts. There was a terrible memory in this part of her life—she pushed it away and continued. Steve got more involved in drinking and taking drugs, but he sure liked his little baby girl. That helped for awhile until Eric was born.

Steve liked Eric, but he was growing tired of family life. He would come and go, never settling down. He started beating Tasha in moments of anger. When her daughter, Valerie, became a teen, he started paying more attention to her. Tasha felt sick inside and pushed all the memories from her mind. Somewhat startled, she found herself back at the Retirement Center sitting in a chair. *Memories—I guess they're not such a comfort after all.*

An elderly gentleman in a wheelchair sat next to Tasha. He was a gruff, grizzly old character whose basic mannerisms was very repulsive, yet Tasha found that she still liked him. She watched him sitting there, half-asleep with saliva draining from the corner of his mouth. Her heart went out to him. No one from his family ever visited him. He must be very lonely. At least she had Eric and Valerie.

"What are you looking at?" he snarled. "Don't you know it's not polite to stare?"

"Sorry," the old woman said. *He is sure hard to get along with,* Tasha thought. "Has your family called?" she asked.

"No!" the old man replied. "Why should they? They have their own lives to live. I don't want them bothering me!"

Tasha was about to answer when the door of the lobby opened and two uniformed men entered. There was no mistaking the style of their uniforms and what they represented.

All the elderly people in the room turned to watch. A complete hush fell on the group as a third man in uniform entered with a wheeled stretcher while the other two checked at the front desk. In the silence the old woman heard a newscaster on the lobby 3-D set reporting that the council was considering a bill that would lower the mandatory termination age from 75 to 72 years.

Tasha shook her head in growing despair. *That one will finish me,* she thought. Then, she barely suppressed a chuckle as she thought, *They certainly are working hard to solve the social security budget problems!*

The three uniformed men rolled the stretcher over next to the old man in the wheelchair.

"What are you doing?" the old man asked. The attendants did not hesitate with the question. They placed their hands on his arms as if to lift him to the mobile stretcher. Surprisingly, the wrinkled old fellow jerked himself free. "I want to know where I am going!" he demanded.

One of the men squatted down next to him. "Listen, old man, all we want to do is take you out for awhile. Don't be afraid."

The elderly gentleman raised himself up to a more erect position in the wheelchair. Wiping the saliva from his mouth, he spoke to the younger man who was still squatted down near him, "Mister, I do not wish to be lied to concerning your intentions."

"All right," was the simple reply. The man lowered his voice to avoid being overheard by others in the room, but it was impossible not to be heard. The whole lounge area was silent—someone had even shut off the 3-D unit. The brooding silence created a threatening atmosphere, even for the three attendants. They felt it, and it made them a little uneasy. The people in the room sensed their discomfort. Meanwhile, Tasha leaned closer and listened.

"Sir," began the young attendant. There was a quality of mercy in his voice. "Your children have requested that you be given rest."

"Why?" the old man responded with a despairing sigh. "I don't ask anything of them. I don't bother them. I've let them have all my money."

The younger man dropped his eyes slightly and said, "They signed the papers for the Lump Sum Clause."

Tasha involuntarily drew in a breath. The Lump Sum Clause allowed family members to cash in a certain amount of money if any social security recipients in their family died before seventy-five. The current laws on retirement stated that anyone over fifty-five had to meet the Quality Of Life (QOL) and Personal Value Tests (PVT). If the person in question failed to meet the minimum viability and productivity standards, then his or her family members had the option of termination.

Just recently, a judge somewhere in New Jersey had ruled that such a decision to terminate did not disqualify the relatives from receiving the lump sum distribution. This was the first time the old woman had seen anyone terminated from her retirement center for this reason. The thought frightened her.

The attendants lifted the old man onto the stretcher and strapped him down. The few moments of dignity he had displayed earlier were now gone. His head was shaking somewhat uncontrollably. "I'm not doing too well," he said. "I'm tired."

Tasha felt her own old age overwhelm her as she watched them roll the whimpering old man out of the lobby.

9:40 a.m.

Tasha felt old as she looked out of her retirement center apartment window at the partly clouded sky. *At least the clouds are free*, she thought. Tasha had given up hope that her daughter would arrive to take her for an outing, so she had returned to her living quarters. She needed the familiar security of her room after watching the incident in the lobby with the old man. She had liked him.

She turned on the 3-D display board, but she wasn't really watching the news. The projected image of the life-sized three-dimensional newsman was reporting that a man, identified only as an anti-freedom terrorist, had broken into a reprocessing plant next to a Reanimation

Center in a nearby city. There seemed to be considerable damage. There was concern that the Third World nations might not receive their proper shipments as a result of the terrorist's actions. His execution was scheduled for later in the afternoon.

The old woman was disturbed, but not over the newscast. A thought had occurred to her which she did not like. *Would Valerie turn me in for the Lump Sum Clause?*

There was a knock at the door, and Tasha shut off the 3-D unit. "You may open the door," she said to the computer. The door slid quietly open. Her daughter, Valerie, walked through, and it closed behind her.

"Dear, you are very late again. What kept you?" Tasha asked. Valerie did not answer because she could find no words to say. She watched as her mother walked over to her, placing her arm around Valerie's shoulder. "I love you," the elderly woman said in a somewhat feeble voice. "It doesn't matter why you were late."

"Mother," Valerie responded, "I've made up my mind. We are going to the Reanimation Center today."

Her mother stepped back and quickly turned her face away from her daughter. The old woman started shaking as her emotions formed a sickening sadness inside of her. She could not get control and found herself blurting out in a sob, "Don't do this."

"You just don't want me to be free to live my own life!" Valerie responded in anger. "You had your chance with no one hanging on to you, keeping you from enjoying the pleasures that I have a right to have. I know what you are thinking inside. You think I'm a murderer for doing the only sensible thing there is to do! How can you be so selfish?!"

61

"You're not a murderer!" Valerie's mother fired back, "But we're talking about life and the right to live! You should not want to take life—any life—no matter how little value it might have!" There was a bitter tone in the old woman's voice as she said the last phrase.

Valerie started to curse but caught herself. Instead she said, "Mother, Master Minh has taught me so much about life and death and the higher level of reality. You won't be dying. You know that. You will be choosing again.

"Try to pick a life you will be happy in," Valerie continued with a note of cynicism. "Anyway, this is my life, my right, and you really have no say in it! Besides, what do you intend to do about it? You have failed the viability tests for several years!" Valerie found herself suddenly exploding with anger as she shouted at her mother, "How dare you say I can't do this! The law is on my side!"

Valerie's mother pulled away. "Don't talk like that to me!" she cried, almost out of control herself.

"Why not?!" Valerie screamed back. "It's proven that humanity must be at a certain level of productivity to enjoy living. If not, they are not considered to be human!"

"I'm human," the old woman said feebly. "Don't you think I am? I hurt, I feel."

"You know what I mean, Mother!" Valerie snapped. Then as if remembering what she was saying a moment before, she spoke with contempt, "Besides, when did you start to worry about what is right and wrong? You haven't been to ritual since father was killed! Why don't you quit fooling yourself?!" Her mother reached out to her again, but Valerie pulled away and stepped back. "Just leave me alone!" The hurt swelled inside the older woman. Tears broke from the corners of her eyes. Her face aged even more as Valerie watched. Then Valerie saw an anger in her mother that she had never seen before.

"Valerie!" her mother cried. "You want to destroy me!" Tasha caught herself before the full force of her wrath broke free. She calmed herself and began to speak softly to her daughter, "Honey, give yourself time to deal with this without making a rash decision you can never undo. I'll do my best to help."

When Tasha reached over to put an arm around her daughter, Valerie roughly pushed her mother away and coldly watched the old woman lose her balance and fall to the floor.

"Oh, Mother," she said and shook her head. "You don't understand." She paused a moment and turned away. "It is no different than what you did to Daddy."

Tasha slowly picked herself up off of the floor and eased onto the couch next to her. Almost ashamed, she spoke to her daughter, "There are other solutions. What about Eric?"

"Yeah," the younger woman replied, "I tried that. He only cares about himself!"

"Don't talk like that," her mother pleaded. "The two of you are better than that." Tasha paused with the reality upon her that her will was weakening. "I just don't want you to do this thing." She stood up and made a motion toward her daughter, as if to make some kind of physical contact. "How can you even allow yourself to consider it?" the old woman continued.

Valerie stepped back, as if afraid of her mother's touch. She felt frustration rising inside her. "I want to be free, Mother. I'm not a young girl anymore. Life is passing me by. I wish to God that I had done this five years ago when you first came to stay with me, but I didn't, and now I want to put it behind me."

Her mother turned away, tears flowing down her old wrinkled cheeks. Allowing herself to sit back down, Tasha spoke in a barely audible voice, "Maybe you are right. If you feel this is the answer, then I can't stop you. Perhaps it's best. I feel like my life doesn't have any purpose anymore."

Valerie felt empty as she walked toward a nearby closet door. She paused, and then faced her mother. The older lady was unable to look her in the face.

"Valerie?" Tasha spoke with bowed head.

"Yes, Mother?"

Her mother answered with a very controlled voice, "Honey, I don't think you know what it means to make the decision you are making. You hate me for what I did with your father, but he was a cruel man...."

"Don't, Mother," Valerie interrupted. "I don't want to hear it."

Tasha continued. "...he killed your twin sister!"

Startled, Valerie said, "I don't have a twin sis—" Horror swept over her. A comment she had once heard her dad say to her about how *he'd do to her what he did to the other one*, came to her mind.

"I'm sorry, Valerie," her mother said. "I was going to tell you about it after we put your father to rest, but I couldn't find the courage. The whole incident was a terrible experience. Your sister was born moments after you, but there was something terribly wrong with her. She was alive, but wasn't moving much.

"The doctor performed a genetic test right in the delivery room while your father paced back and forth by my bed," Tasha continued, her eyes closed as if reliving every vivid detail of the memory. "I remember the doctor ordering all the nurses out as soon as your sister started coming out. I couldn't figure out why at the time. The test showed that your sister had major damage to the brain and would never be able to function normally."

Valerie stood quietly, listening. Her mother was having trouble continuing. "Go on, Mother," Valerie said.

"All right," Tasha said. She took a deep breath and continued, "I will never forget your father's expression when he heard the news about your sister. He asked the doctor how bad, and the doctor said that it would require both of us to commit long hours to her each day. Your father said '*No way.*' He filled a sink full of water there in the room. Then he—" Tasha paused. "—then he picked up your sister and drowned her in it with his own hands. I was too weak to interfere. Now I am ashamed."

Memories began to flood through Tasha's mind— memories of another conversation with her own mother years before. Tears began to flow down the elderly lady's cheeks. After a moment, Tasha said, "The doctor removed your sister's body and signed a stillbirth death certificate. No one ever said anything to us." That was all Tasha's old nerves could handle. She broke into uncontrollable weeping.

Valerie, on the other hand, recovered herself quickly. "Forget it, Mother. There is nothing to be ashamed of." She took her mother's jacket out of the closet and then said casually, "I'll go warm the hover up. It feels a bit chilly outside. I'll be back in a minute." She walked out the door in silence.

Standing alone in the silent room, Tasha spoke softly. "Nothing to be ashamed of? Yes there is, my dear daughter. Years of shame. You never forget."

10:00 a.m.

Karl Harrison walked into his plush administrator's office. The room had an enjoyable fragrance of incense about it. *Hum*, Karl thought, *the sweet smell of success.* He sat down at his desk and activated his data terminal. He deftly manipulated his touch sensor control pad as he rapidly scanned the news headlines. Nothing unusual, other than the terrorist attack on the nearby clinic. Karl smiled with quiet amusement. *I'm pleased to see that it was Harold's clinic that was damaged. He is always getting in my way.*

Here is an interesting article, he thought. Species Preservation authorities had caught a man poaching deer in the Rocky Mountain Park area. He was to be promptly executed the following morning. *Serves him right*, Karl thought. *A civilized society could not allow itself to tolerate the brutal slaying of such a beautiful animal.*

"Tell CaTai," he said to the terminal in front of him, "that I want to see her."

"CaTai is awaiting at her visual terminal," replied an automated but soft feminine voice, "please take your position."

"Thank you," Karl replied, and walked over to a fairly large stage area set into the wall. There were two comfortable rotating seats of the latest fashionable design on the stage, with a state-of-the-art molyresin table between them. On either side of the central chairs were a second set of seats that could only be viewed when one expanded the scan field. Karl walked over and sat down on one of the control chairs.

After a moment had passed, a very lovely oriental women dressed in a business suit appeared in the other chair. *She looks so beautiful,* Karl thought. Her father was an American businessman, and Karl thought that his superior European genetics softened her oriental appearance almost perfectly. He felt the urge to reach out and touch her, but of course that was impossible—the real CaTai was seated in a similar booth halfway around the world.

"How is your weather?" Karl asked.

CaTai smiled. "Making conversation, Karl?"

Karl laughed and said, "Never. How's the weather?"

"Our weather is raging with a hurricane at the moment. What's it like there?"

Karl seized the opportunity. "Sunny and beautiful! Care to fly in for the weekend?" he inquired.

"Sonarflight is a beautiful way to travel," CaTai responded. "However, that bill to prevent termination is scheduled to go on the council floor sometime this weekend. A public servant's work is never done—but somebody's gotta stay home to stop the extremists. I never thought it would get this far. I wish we were like America where the issue was settled. We live in the dark ages here!"

Karl was visibly angry. Why could not people let go of the past? Nevertheless, he smiled and spoke. "Would you like a drink?"

"I could use one," the woman replied as she leaned back in her chair. "The usual," she said.

"Good," Karl interjected as he pushed several buttons on the computer panel. When a champagne glass suddenly appeared filled with liquid, CaTai reached down and picked it up.

"I have a small surprise for you, CaTai—in honor of our second anniversary as...allies," Karl said as he casually ordered himself a drink. "But you must be patient for three more minutes."

As their eyes met, they raised their glasses high in a well-practiced ritual toast.

"To freedom and success and to those who create it—may we get what we deserve!" they said in unison and brought the two glasses together. There was no sound as the two objects passed partially through each other.

Karl spoke, "So the fools finally raised the nerve to put their rantings into a legislative bill? How dare they say we don't have the right to practice termination. The terminal option is the most sane social policy ever developed. It is our mandate for exisistence at the SBI! Our administration of the right of option has prevented over-population; it allows humans to experience their fullest potential, and it has almost stopped suffering and pain. Do they want to go back to that?"

"I don't understand it either," CaTai sighed. "Listen, I have got to go."

Karl leaned forward suddenly and said, "CaTai—I have the *solution* to your problem with the Council." At the same time, he modified his viewscreen to wide scan, knowing CaTai would be able to see both seats at his location.

Karl watched with amusement as CaTai visibly stiffened her pose, irritation and doubt clouding her face. "Karl, your ego is second to none, I can respect and even envy that," CaTai said. "But to claim you have the solution to such a complex problem is ludicrous...and why have you put this little infant on the seat beside you? We both know you loath them as irritating nuisances. I'm sorry, but you know I can't bear to be toyed with."

Karl seemed to lean even closer, "CaTai, if you have learned anything about me over the last 24 months, you have learned that I do nothing unless there is design, reason and profit in it. This is no different."

"But why...?" CaTai asked.

"Two years ago I laid out a simple plan to show the European Council the error of their ways," Karl said in intense tones. "I told you to use the money angle. You asked me to prove it would work...

"...*this* (as he nods toward the blond-haired two-year old boy sitting almost motionless on the third chair) is my proof."

CaTai awkwardly shifted position in her seat and nervously drained her champagne glass. "I'm sorry Karl. Maybe I'm not as brilliant or devious as you are, but I'm getting tired of these games."

Karl slowly shook his head, allowing a controlled grin to appear across his face as he replied, "CaTai, you'll like this game well enough after it makes you the most powerful woman on the European Council!"

CaTai regained her composure and took a few moments to refresh herself with two tabs from her RecDrug kit before looking up at Karl with an amused grin, "Karl, I hate you. You always know how to get past my anger— and I really do hate you for it. Well, go on. I know you'll do it anyway."

"Exactly," said Karl. "This boy is yours, CaTai."

The silence became menacing and obvious in its intensity.

"Perhaps I should say—ours," Karl continued after a long pause. I'm sure you remember looking at it in a quartz lab cube about two years ago in my office? I decided it would make a good momento and memorial to document our association in this new venture..."

"Why would you...? CaTai answered before being cutoff as Karl relentlessly pursued his line of logic.

"CaTai, this is the answer to the sniveling anti-option sectors of your opposition on the Council. My studies show they have a historical, if not "spiritual," attraction to extreme nationalism, even a type of inherited preference for gene-selected social progress.

"It is simple," Karl continued, obvious warming to his subject. "Give them something they want—advanced gene-splicing technology and heriditary testing protocols to *improve their race or national gene pool*, and they will quickly give in to your demands for total freedom in reproductive options."

CaTai was the one who leaned forward this time, "Are you telling me you are willing to sell me equipment and technology from the Reanimation Institute—even though it will bring the Council economic equity?"

"Of course," Karl replied, as he narrowed the scan focus to his seat alone. "I have no loyalty but to myself. Why should I? Besides, this technology is valuable medical research which must be shared for the good of viable mankind. And you and I can make a lot of money on it."

"You're sure it will convince the anti-option factions to let the Termination bill pass the Council vote tomorrow?"

"They'll change their votes so fast you'll have a whole new view of our splendid human species, CaTai. Think about it: they have to let it pass. *It is based on the same logic base they must use to launch their new 'commercial genetic development and nurturing' industry.*"

CaTai settled back in her seat with a sigh, "I need another drink, Karl. I hope you're right on this thing. There are so many details to cover…"

Karl motioned toward her drink and raised his for another toast, "I've already taken care of the details,

CaTai. You will receive a security dispatch within five minutes which will contain all the necessary papers and background information.

"Included with these are the names and security clearance codes for five top flight researchers and termination/genetic technicians who are waiting in Brussels at this very moment with all the equipment necessary to set up the first state-of-the-art Reanimation and Genetic Research Center outside of American borders. Consider this as a downpayment on my—I mean our very lucrative retirement…" Karl said.

CaTai shook her head and drained her glass, "I have a lot of study to do before tomorrow arrives. If this thing works out—let's try for the following weekend, okay?"

"Sounds good to me!" Karl said, "bye!"

"Goodby!" the woman said as she faded from sight.

Karl looked over at the boy in the seat beside him and said, "I hope you're worth the gamble. You know what happens if you aren't, don't you?"

The two year old seemed to comprehend the words. After darting a fearful glance at the open veranda with its magnificent high-rise view of the city, he silently slipped off the chair and toddled out of the room under the man's silent stare.

Chapter Five

Valerie helped her mother, Tasha, through the wide double doors of the Reanimation Center. She eased the older woman down into one of the comfortable waiting chairs, next to another elderly lady. Then she went up to the front desk.

Tasha sat quietly, immersed in her own thoughts. She was only occasionally aware of Valerie answering the necessary questions. She wasn't interested in most of the conversation, but one question did catch her attention. The nurse asked Valerie if she wished to use the termination option on herself as well.

"Are you crazy?" Valerie responded. "I have a lot of living I still want to do!"

After that, Tasha was not very interested in what else was said. She was in the middle of her memories when the older woman next to her spoke.

"Is that one your only daughter?" the lady asked.

"Yes," Tasha replied. "Do you have any children?"

"Oh, yes, a son!" the other woman perked up. "He is the kindest man...was the kindest man you could ever meet."

"What happened to him?" Tasha asked. She felt she already knew the answer.

"They just took him in to be laid to rest. My turn will be soon."

Tasha felt sorry for the elderly lady. "Who signed your papers?" she asked.

There was a quiet pause before the answer came. "My grandson is very busy enjoying his life. There was no time for us."

"I'm sorry," Tasha shared with real feeling.

The other woman shook her head. "Don't feel sorry for me. I intend to be brave. They say it isn't bad. They claim it is quite painless. They even play your favorite music to help put you to sleep."

"We are going to die," Tasha said. "I am afraid."

Valerie walked over and stood in front of her mother. She felt a little shaky, but she felt she owed her mother at least a good-by.

"Well?" Tasha said to her daughter. There was an unmistakable sound of bitterness in her voice.

"Good-by, Mother," the younger woman said. Her mother turned her head and did not answer. A moment passed, and Valerie turned to leave.

"Don't go!" Tasha pleaded. "Let me live."

"I've signed the papers, Mother," Valerie snapped back. "They wouldn't let you go now—even if I asked."

Her mother started sobbing. Valerie felt the tears begin to flow down her own cheeks too. *What had she done?* She looked at the nurse behind the desk. The uniformed woman who stood there saw her wavering look. She walked over and took Valerie by the arm and then escorted her to the door.

"It's all right," the nurse said. "Go home and rest. We'll take care of everything."

Valerie walked through the door into the sunlight. The sun on her face seemed to break her depression. She shook the despair from her mind. She knew she had done the right thing. She was free at last. It was only fair. It was her legal right!

11:45 a.m.

Overwhelmed with despair, Tasha's bent old body sat quietly in the beautifully decorated office of Karl Harrison. She was trying to understand why she was still alive. The nurse had called her name and as she followed, the uniformed woman had led her past the entrance to the termination room. She had caught a glimpse of the elderly lady she had spoken with in the waiting room being seated in a reclining chair. A machine was being hooked up to her. Then the door closed as Tasha walked by. The nurse then led her into this lovely office and left her.

Karl Harrison entered rather briskly into the room, giving Tasha somewhat of a start. He looked and acted very professional, but there was kindness in his voice as he spoke.

"Hello," he said. "Sorry to have kept you waiting—" A humorous thought came to Tasha's mind, but she felt no urge to express it. "—but I had to complete last-minute arrangements to send off a two-year-old," Harrison said.

Noting the old woman's raised eyebrows, he casually explained, "I sent the kid off to the Osaka Leadership Youth Academy...I should have been so lucky." Then he sat down behind the desk and began sifting through some papers.

Tasha watched for a moment, then found that she could stand the suspense no longer. "Why am I still alive?" she asked.

Karl looked up and smiled. "Mrs. Jones," he began, "I have been reviewing your records. Everything seems to be in order, Lump Sum Clause benefit distribution and all. However, the data center informs me you have a private account with twenty thousand credits in it. Your daughter is obviously not aware of this account. She failed to list it with your assets to be transferred to her ownership—something she would not fail to do if she knew it existed. Without these assets being assigned, the federal government will take them."

"She does not know of them," Tasha said quietly.

"Why did you keep it a secret from your daughter, Mrs. Jones?" Karl asked. "Were you planning to use them to—shall we say—escape?" Tasha thought that he had such a charming smile.

"Yes," she answered.

"That is what I thought," he said. Karl leaned back in his chair and continued. "Mrs. Jones, may I call you Tasha?"

"Yes," the old woman responded.

"Thank you. Tasha, what would you say if I told you that you could still use those credits to escape?" Tasha noted that he clearly emphasized the word, escape.

"I would be very interested," she replied. "But how?"

Karl leaned forward and explained with genuine enthusiasm, "It is really very simple. We substitute a transient from the streets for you in the termination chamber. The body will be labeled as yours at the processing plant. We have to keep the books balanced, and the government inspectors keep strict tabs on the body count. For the right price, however, they pay very little attention to body identification."

Tasha felt a slight glimmer of hope as she asked, "How will you get me out?"

"There is a hidden panel in the termination chamber. As soon as the nurse leaves, my friends will bring in the unconscious substitute and will take you to safety. It will be a long process, but we have a hidden village up in the mountains where you will be able to live out your life in peace. Here, let me show you."

Karl reached into his desk drawer and pulled out a small photo album. He plugged it into his terminal and the room seemed to transform itself into a beautiful village nestled on a far-off mountainside. Tasha watched as life-like 3-D figures of elderly people walked by in total contentment. They were laughing and joking. They seemed so much at peace.

"It is beautiful," Tasha's now hopeful voice whispered. "I want to go there."

"You can—I promise," Karl said enthusiastically as he shut off the album. The room became as it was before. "You must understand that such a place costs a great deal of money to maintain. That is why we need your twenty thousand credits. That is how we fund the project." Karl leaned back, very pleased with himself.

Tasha thought for a moment of the poor wretched woman who would take her place. She felt some guilt and regret, but she also very much wanted to live. "What do I have to do?" she asked in a determined tone.

Karl Harrison stood up, walked over to Tasha, and handed her a numbered sensor pad of the latest design.

"What is this?" she asked.

"I believe you know what it is. Key in the private access code for your account," he said. "Be sure to use your index finger so the bank's body scan unit will register that it is you. We'll do the rest."

Tasha reached for the sensor pad. Slowly, her wrinkled, feeble finger tapped out the access code. When she was through, she handed the keyboard back to Karl. He double-checked the information, entered a couple more commands and set the tiny sensor pad down on his desk. A moment passed, and a smile crossed his lips. After touching a flush-mounted sensor switch under the arm of his plush office chair, he turned to Tasha.

"Trust me," Karl Harrison said. "You have been open and fair with me. I'll get you through this. You have nothing to fear. Just do as you are told," and then he turned away.

A nurse immediately entered the room and led Tasha Jones to the same termination chamber she'd seen earlier. The other old woman was nowhere to be seen. The nurse mechanically strapped Tasha's arms and legs to the padded reclining chair.

"Why do you do that if it doesn't hurt?" Tasha asked. The nurse ignored her and silently finished the task of preparing her. Then she left. The room was completely quiet. Tasha could not hear a sound. Seconds passed, and soft music began to play.

When will the panel open? Tasha wondered.

She found herself growing very sleepy. It was impossible to stay awake. Her thoughts traveled to a country road where she saw herself as a teenager riding a bicycle. She watched the accident and felt the pain as she stood up and looked over the damaged two-wheeler. Then she turned and saw Jeff standing there, but he wasn't young anymore. Neither was she. However, he was as handsome as always, and Tasha felt beautiful herself. Jeff reached out and took her by the arm. They began walking through a beautiful village on a far-off mountain. She saw herself standing very close to him, laughing, and suddenly they were both young and happy again.

A storm was forming over the village. Everything was grey. Her thoughts were breaking apart. The village was fading.

When will the panel open?

Silence. Darkness. Quiet.

Terror. Panic.

Stillness.

Betrayal.

Death.

PART III

Final

Year 2106
(54 years later)

Chapter Six

4:45 a.m.

Everything was dark. Maria sat with her eyes open—unable to see anything as she stared into the gloom around her. She didn't like the fact that she seemed to live in unending darkness. It left her with a feeling of unknown terror that she couldn't seem to shake. She wanted very much to spend more time on the surface, but most of the time they were not allowed to go outside.

It felt damp and cold where she sat. In a moment of self-pity, Maria felt the tattered clothes she wore and her mind flowed naturally back to the outdoors. The color of her brown military-style shirt and khaki campaign shorts had shown gray in the twilight when she'd left the burrow the previous evening.

It had felt so lonely, but peaceful, to walk in the faded light of that dying sunset. How she loved being outside! She wondered what it would be like to wear beautiful clothes and live in a house that was her own.

The children never got to go outside. Maria was ashamed of her selfishness.

Shivering in the pre-dawn chill, Maria moved her assault weapon off of her lap, leaned it against her shoulder with the barrel pointing up, and pulled her knees to her chest. Below her in the lower end of the darkness, some of the children stirred restlessly. After a moment, they fell back into a fitful sleep.

I feel very alone right now, she thought, *but not as alone as those poor kids.* There was tension in her young, slim body, and strength too. With a conscious effort, she was able to relax her muscles. Her youthful face turned in the direction of a sound near the entrance—she heard someone coming.

That will be Paul, she hoped. *It's time for him to relieve me on guard duty.* She was right. Paul came in with a flashlight and sat down next to her.

"Hi, Sunshine!" he whispered softly. "Everything quiet?"

Maria smiled at the young man next to her. "Yes, everything is quiet," she said. "The children are a little restless, but who could blame them. All they have ever known is danger, darkness and hiding." She leaned her head against his shoulder. "I'm glad you're here. I've been feeling very lonely all night."

Paul carefully layed his weapon against the hard surface of the floor—pointing it away from the children, and put his arm around her. Reaching down, he shut the flashlight off. "I heard about your brother. He was a brave man to sacrifice himself so those children could escape. I'm really sorry, Maria. I know it hurts."

Maria felt her heart break at the mention of her brother. She had maintained herself all evening, but now she couldn't hold it in any longer. She started sobbing.

"I'm sorry," Paul said. "I shouldn't have said anything."

"It's OK," she told him. "I have been holding it in, and I need to let it out." She wiped her eyes and spoke again. "He knew the risks. I just wish that he hadn't died that way." She stopped a moment, then asked, "Is his body still hanging from that building?"

"I don't know," Paul answered. He looked down wishing he could see the pretty features of her face. He breathed a small sigh. "It's terrible to feel so trapped. Sometimes, Maria, I feel like there is no way out. It has gone too far."

Maria nestled her head against Paul's shoulder. She felt secure next to him and enjoyed the sense of his strength and warmth. They had promised each other that when this was over, they would be married. It made no sense while the war was being fought.

The State Bureau of Investigation was vicious, and death was a common thing. The SBI's organization had unlimited investigation rights as well as total enforcement power. It was so risky to care for another person. Maria closed her eyes as if to blot out horrible images that flowed in front of her. It did no good.

Painful memories drifted slowly through her mind, leaving her with an overwhelming sense of sadness. Her parents had been law-abiding citizens who felt strongly about the preservation of all human life. They came from a devoted family of believers in western Canada.

Maria let her mind continue to wander. Her great grandfather, Jeff Fay, had moved to that area of Canada about a hundred years ago, shortly after the turn of the twenty-first century. His story was somewhat of a dramatic one. Marie's mother told her that her great grandfather left the United States in despair over a girl he loved who had chosen to abort his child.

For years, Fay never dated or considered marriage. He worked hard and saved up enough money to buy a large piece of land to build a home on. About a year later, he met a beautiful Canadian girl who was a Christian and they were soon married. For Jeff Fay, the past became just that—the past. The couple had four sons and a charming daughter. Maria's grandmother was that daughter.

Maria loved to think of her family history. Its storybook quality gave her hope that someday her life might be like that. She dreamed of sharing a home and family with Paul.

Reality was a different story. When abortion took the new terrible turns of cruelty that now existed, Maria's parents joined the armed resistance to try to stop it. In the early years of the twenty-first century, Canada surprised everyone by voting as a nation to ban abortion. Many Canadians crossed the border into the United States to get their abortions, and many Americans fled to Canada to be free to live godly lives. Canada became one of the few countries in the world without termination laws.

As the century moved to its midway point, tension grew between the two countries, and the borders were closed. Under emergency measures, the United States government formed a "Grand Council," linking it with other nations who shared its twisted views on life and death. An "underground railroad" was set up in Canada to help rescue people trapped in the growing web of death south of the border.

Maria's parents became deeply involved in the movement. They were assigned to a hidden refuge center in the United States. The resistance used refuge centers such as theirs to shelter children who had been rescued before an abortion, along with unwed mothers and elderly people.

Both Maria and her brother were there when their parents were killed in a violent SBI raid on the refuge center. The two siblings had no time to weep for their mom and dad because it was all they could do to avoid being caught. They were able to hide in the vent system with some of the other children. From that day on, they were raised in Canada under the protection of the underground railroad. Together, they decided to return to the United States and help rescue others as their parents had done.

Just before they left the safety of the Canadian border, Maria discovered a whole new area of life. It happened one spring morning when she entered the mess tent for breakfast. She had just turned sixteen, and she had no thoughts about dating. Her mind was centered on the horrors in America instead of on the boys in the camp.

Her brother often teased her about it, saying she would never get married that way. She just ignored him.

This morning was different. She spotted the young man sitting by himself the moment she walked in the tent. She was not sure why he first caught her attention. Perhaps it was because of the lonely way he sat apart from everyone else. She asked around and discovered that he was new to Canada. When she learned that his parents had just been killed in a rescue in Oregon, her heart went out to him immediately. Maria amazed herself by taking her plate of food over to his table and sitting down across from the young stranger.

"Hello," she said with a smile. "My name is Maria. What's yours?"

"Paul," came the quiet response.

"Are you going to be here long?" she asked in a soft, unintruding voice.

Paul shrugged his shoulders. "I don't know. I just got here this morning. They haven't even told me where I'll sleep." He went quiet and looked down at his food.

Maria was not sure what to say next. She decided that honesty was always right, so she shared, "I'm glad you're here. I'd like to be your friend if you'll let me."

Paul looked up with a grateful expression on his face. "Thanks," he told her. "I could use a friend. Things have not been easy the last few weeks." A tear formed at the edge of his right eye, but he would not acknowledge it. He smiled at Maria and added, "I'm glad you're here, also."

Maria's memories were suddenly interrupted, and the "living now" forced itself upon her. One of the children started crying and she quickly made her way over to him. Paul helped her see by shining the light of the flashlight on the ceiling. She picked up the little three-year-old boy, carried him over next to Paul, and sat down with the child resting on her lap. He whimpered slightly but soon fell back to sleep. Maria enjoyed holding this child for he was special to her. She had nicknamed him, Blessed, because he was almost left behind at a rescue.

Looking down at Blessed's soft smile, Maria whispered, "I'm glad I was there." Paul nodded his head gently in agreement. He knew the story. Maria had been present when the boy was rescued.

It happened during a night operation at a place called the New Hope Clinic. The facility only did the Class I abortions because it was not licensed for the more federally regulated Class II procedures in the Reanimation Centers. The security for such a small place was very relaxed. Maria and her brother and four others worked their way carefully through the security alarm system and into the storage warehouse.

Once they were inside, the rescuers began transporting the lightweight PAWs units to a hidden truck. PAWs stood for "Portable Artificial Wombs," cocoon-like structures that were about the size of a large handbag. They were designed to keep the unborn "fetus" existence sustained and fully functional "for experimentation and commercial purposes."

Everyone who worked in rescues had a basic understanding of how the PAWs units worked. They were self-contained machines that rested in battery charging cradles. When a PAWs unit was lifted from its resting place, it would automatically disconnect itself from the charger. The battery indicator light would change from green to red indicating that the unit was functioning normal on battery power. Only if something went wrong would the light start flashing red.

After each rescue, the PAWs were taken to a secret refuge center where they were put on chargers to continue life support until the children inside were able to function on their own.

Maria and the others had removed nearly half of the PAWs when the alarm system went off. They began an insane scramble to grab as many of the units as possible and escape. Maria was carrying four as she ran from the building to their hidden truck. The weight was exhausting her strength, and she stumbled just as an SBI patrol car pulled up. She managed to grab three of the units and crawl to the truck without being discovered. Then she turned to go back for the last lonely cocoon resting on the grass.

More police units pulled up, but Maria did not stop. She crawled on her belly in the open, praying that she would not be discovered. Flashlights shined all over and officers passed near her, but no one saw her.

Maria finally managed to locate the lost PAWs unit, but when she looked for the truck, it was not there. She understood why. The others could not wait for her and have all of them caught. Her brother was in charge—it must have been a tough decision. Maria looked down at the tiny boy in the incubator and made him a promise: *I'll get you to safety*, she spoke in silence. *I won't leave you.*

Maria kept her promise—even though it took four days of hiding and desperate travel on foot to make it safely back to the refuge center.

Paul loved Maria, but he would also always respect her. She had tremendous courage. He looked at her in the dim light of the flashlight as it reflected off of the ceiling. She seemed so natural holding Blessed in her arms. "What are you thinking?" he asked.

Maria spoke softly, "It makes me angry that every one of these children would have been aborted by their mothers. What have we become?"

"Ungodly is all I can think to say," Paul replied. "I only hope they can get these children to Canada without being caught. Your brother almost made it to the border with his group before...there's a leak in the network there. We are going to have to be careful." He paused a moment, then said, "Number Seven will be here today."

"That will mean there will be another raid." Maria held the little boy close to her.

Paul nodded. "Yes, I believe you're right." The two of them sat quietly next to each other with the child sleeping contentedly in the girl's arms.

Maria's mind moved toward thoughts of Canada once again. She had spent about ten years there. It was such a beautiful place. How strange, she thought, that a nation that had started out almost as evil as her own in the killing of unborn children had made such a reversal. She was glad that it was at least one of the few nations on earth that took a pro-life stand.

The United States and Canada were so different. They now existed continually in a near state of war. Because of that, Canada was rapidly building its defensive weaponry in case of attack. Everyone felt certain that the United States would not tolerate Canada's position much longer.

"Is it all right if I stay here?" Maria asked. "I don't feel like going back with the others right now. I just want to be near you."

"Sure, Sunshine," Paul replied and put his arm around her shoulder. "I could really use the company myself. Besides, we don't want to wake the kid."

"Thanks."

Maria closed her eyes. Morning seemed a long way away. They sat there quietly for awhile, deep in their thoughts with the flashlight shining on the ceiling. Then Paul startled Maria with a very strange statement.

"We must not be full yet," he said.

"What?!" she asked with a definite surprised tone in her voice.

"I said, we must not be full yet," he responded.

Maria sat up from her leaning position. The little boy stirred restlessly in her arms. "What are you talking about?" she asked with an inquisitive look. She had learned long before that Paul was a deep thinker and usually did not say anything without a purpose.

"The Amorites," he said.

"The who?"

Paul looked at her and smiled. He spoke patiently. "The Amorites—their civilization—if you can call it that—existed thousands of years ago in the Middle East Sector....

"What about them?"

"I had some spare time at base camp last week," Paul replied. "so I read a few chapters from my Bible...when I read about the Amorites I began to understand why the Grand Council banned the Bible as subversive contraband and exempted it from all "freedom of speech" amendments and provisions...."

Paul looked across at the sleeping children. "God promised the Jews a land, but He told them that He wouldn't give it to them right away because *the iniquity* of the current inhabitants—the Amorites—*was not yet full.*

"I guess God wanted to give them as much time as possible to repent, but in the end God used His people to destroy their nation. I guess the sin of America is not yet full enough for God to destroy it.

"I wonder where the line really is for America? When will God say 'It is enough'?"

Maria looked out across the children as well and said, "I'd say we are very close."

"Yes," Paul agreed with Maria. "It is enough. In the twentieth century, Christians talked continually about the Lord's return. They thought the second coming would be the solution of all problems, that it would stop all evil. Yet, it did not happen.

"When the abortion issue first was fought in the nineteen hundreds, it was still possible to turn the tide," Paul continued with a hint of pain in his voice, "but many Christians just stood by and watched. It wasn't that they were cowards—at least I don't think so. They wanted to be honest and not break the laws, and I think they hoped that God would take them out of this world before things got worse.

"I believe that Jesus Christ could come at any time and take those that have trusted in Him back to heaven," Paul said, "but I have no guarantee that it will be soon. We as a people praise the Lord continually, and we certainly have more reason to believe it will happen in our lifetime than in any other, but what if it doesn't?

"Today, I think those believers in the last century would say it is a God-given responsibility to face reality and stand for what is right," Paul said. "I think Christians have always been expected to hope for His coming and face tribulation for His Name."

Maria looked up with tears in her eyes. Blessed started to stir again, so she laid him carefully next to her as Paul watched, looking a little embarrassed.

"Sorry," he said. "I didn't mean to get so worked up."

Paul looked down at his feet, feeling self-conscious. "It's just that I get these thoughts boiling over in my head and no one to express them to—except you."

"I'll take that as a compliment," Maria said, as she moved a little closer to him for warmth in the damp room.

"Maria," he began again. "I keep asking myself how we ended up hiding in holes and risking our lives to save children and elderly people…it's crazy!!

Paul paused a moment, and then said, "I do think God will judge America if it does not repent.

"This thing didn't start with abortion. It began when our *modern* society as a whole concluded God was not absolute in His laws and questioned His existence. They tucked Him safely away in a religious corner for those they thought were extremist and made truth relative. If God is not the absolute authority for society, then *man becomes the final authority* with absolute power. Once that happens, Maria," Paul continued, "the unthinkable is possible."

Suddenly, a young girl about twelve years old moved toward them with quick, quiet movements. She squatted down next to them and whispered, "Code E!", then turned and moved on. Paul and Maria went into instant action. Somewhere in the refuge center SBI agents were making a raid! Maria pulled a special roll of tape from her backpack and she and Paul began to tape the children's mouths as they woke them up. None of the twenty or so boys and girls seemed frightened by the action for it had been practiced many times in their young lives.

"Maria," Paul whispered, "take the children and get them to the designated hiding place. I'll join you as soon as I can. I need to see if the others need help."

Maria nodded as she finished tying a soft rope securely around the last child. Paul had already disappeared, so she turned and starting leading her young caravan off through the underground tunnels. It did not take Maria very long to realize that the raid was massive. She found herself dodging SBI patrols everywhere. She was very frightened but knew she could not let the children sense it. Despair began to set in when she discovered that the hiding place area was under SBI control.

Where to now? Maria asked God in a silent prayer. There was only one solution and that was to head for Emergency Shelter Three—but that meant going above ground and moving on the surface. Normally that was considered too dangerous, but with the hallways filled with SBI patrols, it didn't make much difference. "Come on," she whispered to the children. They were well trained, and they obediently followed.

Before long, Maria found the hidden stairway and carried the children to the surface one by one. The situation above ground was just as bad if not worse. SBI hovercopters were flying everywhere. Maria bit her lower lip. This wasn't going to be easy.

A terrifying hour passed as Maria worked her way through the back streets with the children. They had almost been spotted several times but somehow had escaped detection. She knew the children were tired and would not be able to keep this up much longer. As for herself, she was exhausted. She did not know where her strength was coming from, but she kept going and prayed that Paul was all right.

When they finally reached the hidden entrance of Emergency Shelter Three, Maria started to open the ground level door when a gruff voice behind her shouted, "Freeze! Nobody move!"

Maria turned and saw a SBI patrolman about fifteen feet from her with his laser pistol pointed directly at her. Maria's mind raced for an idea, but none came. She slowly stood up with raised hands.

The officer continued speaking. "You are under arrest for the theft and illegal transportation of state property!"

Where was Paul? Maria desperately needed help. She measured the distance between her and the patrolman. No chance to jump him.

"Under Treasury Ruling 2417," the SBI agent stated looking directly at Maria, "you are to be taken immediately to the nearest Reanimation Center for termin—…"

"No, she's not!" came a voice from behind the patrolman. The officer whirled to fire on this new threat when a laser blast hit him full in the chest. He fell at Maria's feet. The helmet that covered his head rolled off revealing a young man about twenty years of age. He was very much dead. Maria felt sorry for him, but there was no time for regrets. Paul ran up beside her.

"Get the children inside," he ordered. "I'll take care of this guy. Hurry!" She quickly did what she was told— she had no choice.

6:25 a.m.

Number Seven leaned over the railing of his high-rise apartment balcony hung 105 stories above the city below. It always gave him a dizzy feeling, and he wasn't really sure why he did it. He couldn't stay in this position looking down at the street without experiencing an insane fear that someone was coming up behind him to toss him over the edge.

Frowning at the phobia that had haunted him from childhood, Number Seven took a step back and stared across the building tops that stretched to the horizon. Daylight was just beginning to appear as the sun tried to thread its rays through the maze of buildings in front of him.

His eyes followed the movement of the light until they came to a stop on the towering SBI building downtown. Anger exploded inside of him! Number Seven sat down in a reclining chair on the balcony and continued to watch the sunlight play on the sprawling city below. Waves of anger surged through him—how could he bear this disappointment at belonging to the human race?

All about him were man's great achievements. Space travel to Mars, the new light ray transporter recently developed which even now was being used to beam people all over—these and many other science fiction realities of modern times were signs that man was on the edge of his own human greatness.

Medicine had cured many diseases. *Still*, Number Seven thought, *there were so many new ones—H.S.-23 was the latest threat to humanity.* Known as "Hormone Sickness," H.S.-23 was another sexually transmitted disease that caused extreme changes in its host, creating a basic rotting of the human body. There was no known cure and death came within weeks of the first symptoms. Not since the AIDS scare at the turn of the previous century had a disease received so much attention.

Number Seven breathed a sigh of sadness. None of this was important. A society that spent billions on curing a death-dealing sexually transmitted disease just to continue its immoral life style—while not hesitating to kill its offspring and elderly—was beyond pity.

"What have we become?" Number Seven asked his God as he leaned forward placing his head in his hands. "Where is your judgment? I would rather you rain fire from heaven upon this nation killing all of us than to let this murder of the innocent go on!"

These periods of anger he felt came and went. *At least America is not as bad as Europe*, he thought. Death was something of a hobby there. Coliseums were being reopened and the ancient Roman games were being enacted once again, this time with television cameras and instant replays. The carnage that was taking place was beyond imagination. Further east, Asian leaders were making decisions concerning life that were staggering. To solve population problems, they had decided on mandatory termination at age fifty. Number Seven sadly thought of the millions of children butchered in America before the war on abortion had truly begun.

He had to admit that he felt anger at the people of the previous century who had taken too long to break free of their apathy and a false sense of loyalty to a government that destroyed human lives in such a casual way.

He tried hard to forgive, though. They had simply not understood until it was too late.

Number Seven walked over to the balcony and once again leaned over the rail until the nausea and dizziness nearly overwhelmed him. Today, men and women under his leadership would be risking their lives. He silently whispered the motto and desperate prayer of his organization—*God save the children!*

Chapter Seven

7:05 a.m.

Rachel Morgan stood in the full glare of sunlight bursting through her penthouse window with outstretched arms, enjoying the warmth radiating through the glass. *Today is going to be a beautiful day,* she thought. Victory is always beautiful, and today would be victorious. At thirty-five years of age, she was stunningly beautiful, and she knew it. *It is fun,* Rachel thought, *to be stunningly beautiful and know it*! Every man she knew wanted her to belong to him, but it was always on her terms. She had seen to that.

Rachel turned toward her computer. She had a call to make. After saying a couple of verbal commands, she saw the face of a young man appear in the room before her. When she had executed two motion commands, the computer brought the rest of his body into sight. He was reclining on a sofa and looked up casually. "Hello, Rachel," he said. "Is there anything I can do for you?"

"Yes!" Rachel responded. "I am about to achieve a great victory in my developing career. Would you like to join me here this evening to celebrate my success?"

The young man smiled. "If you would like me to come, you know I will."

Rachel paused a moment in thought. This would be a time to really celebrate. "Robert," she said.

"Yes?"

Rachel spoke softly, "Bring your sister."

The young man dropped his eyes but nodded in agreement. "If that is what you want."

Rachel ignored Robert's lack of enthusiasm. "See you both this evening!" She spoke in a casual way as she shut off the screen. Robert's jealous possessiveness amused her, but she was used to having her own way in every-thing—in physical relationships, in friendships, and now…in her career!

Some people think I am terribly self-centered, Rachel thought and then chuckled inwardly. *Well, I am! Actually, I'm quite special!* That is what her mother always told her. Her mother had had seven abortions before deciding that Rachel was to be born. The doctor's test had proven that she would be a perfect baby with absolutely no flaw. The new genetic test had shown she would be of supreme intelligence.

Once, Rachel had felt sorry for the other seven unborn brothers and sisters. Her mother had beaten her severely for such a reaction. "They were nothing," she had said. "They were sub-life. They were never human. You are an only child!" Rachel would never forget her mother. As for her father, the thought of him never crossed her mind.

Rachel Morgan glanced at her watch. It was time to head to her office across the city. She felt disgust—even bitterness—at the thought of moving through traffic to get to work. She would be more than happy if the Translight really could provide intercity transmission soon. She welcomed any device or advancement which allowed her to live her life without interference—*people are so annoying*, she thought. She hoped that it would happen in the next year or two as promised. Meanwhile, Translight at least made world travel more bearable.

As Rachel stepped on to the sidewalk amidst the busy crowd, she caught a glimpse of a mother and daughter walking together holding each other's hands. *That's a sight I don't see very often nowadays*, she thought. Abortion was making children much more scarce. Suddenly, she felt an involuntary pain of regret as her mind flashed back to her most recent abortion. The fetus was in the sixth cycle when her I.Q. level registered below Rachel's requirements.

Rachel quickly shook off the unwelcome thought. People said she was overly picky, but Rachel intended to raise just one child, and that child would have to be as special as that child's mother was. The abortion had been the sensible thing to do—and most important of all—it was her right! Rachel quickly pushed the lingering feelings of regret aside as she moved toward the public transportation centers.

7:35 a.m.

Tabitha stood above the cliff overlooking the great lake beneath her. She watched the light of the multi-colored sunrise grow brighter as daylight became a part of the morning. The sunlight gave her warmth as she stood feeling the breeze of the lake blowing gently in her face—yet her heart was cold.

She was angry and sensed a bitterness that she could not explain. She wondered if it might well be from the voice inside her, the being that walked with her. Her temper was very much hers though, and she sensed no regret with that. If the world or anyone in it made her angry, she believed she was fully justified in striking back. The entity within agreed, and she was comforted by that thought.

Sometimes, Tabitha found herself so deep in despair that there was only darkness left. During those times, even her spiritual companion was unable to help. There could be no escaping the night that surrounded her soul—Tabitha knew that any moment of freedom from her depression was just temporary deliverance. The despair would engulf her again.

She sighed. She had learned to live with it. Why couldn't she be like her Grandma, Valerie Jones, who had never married and had been fiercely independent? She had been able to terminate several of her fetuses without any guilt.

"The fetus is just an extension of your body," Grandma had said. "Removing it is like removing an unwanted tax burden. In fact it is. The government taxes people for children nowadays!"

Tabitha shook her head with the memory. She did not feel that her fetus was a tax burden. Even with the sleepless nights of the early cycles, she'd felt at least a temporary sense of completeness. Later on in her life—when she was ready—it might be the fulfilment of a dream. Now, this fetus was only causing her to feel frustrated with her own burdened existence.

She knew she was thinking freely only because the presence within was not active at the moment. *Grandma would not have tolerated that kind of thinking*, Tabitha thought to herself. She remembered as a child sitting and listening as Valerie Jones would share with her the principles of life and reincarnation.

"Tabitha," her grandmother would say, "the real you, what some people call your soul, has chosen this life you are living. There is no right or wrong in it. There is only existence. When you die, your life force will search out another existence. Choose wisely and learn from this time. Never be afraid of reaching your goal even if you slow down the progress of others. Harmony comes from control of oneself. Take control of your life and never let another life force interfere. They must either learn or regress. Be strong and brave or the universe will leave you behind, and you will be nothing."

The waves below Tabitha were not very large, but they were relaxing to watch. The breeze had softened some taking the chill away. Inside, Tabitha knew the truth of her feelings. The fetus would have to be aborted because it did not fit into her future plans. She supposed she should have thought of that earlier, but she had not.

Grandma would have said, "Don't let the little critter get in your way of enjoying life." Poor Grandma, she seemed pretty depressed when she contracted H.S.-23. The virus had been in her for many years before it became active. Without warning, Grandma just shriveled up and died. Tabitha had felt much better after Mother shared that it had not been such a great tragedy after all, since Grandma was near the age of mandatory termination anyway.

Tabitha wondered if Grandma had decided on her next life yet. How long would it be before the old woman moved on from this plane of existence?

Tabitha longed for new horizons. Europe seemed to be the location her spirit wanted to experience. There was so much freedom there without America's restrictive inhibitions left over from the last century. Human "morality" was such an unnatural and confining thing.

She sighed again and turned her back on the brilliant light that the sun was now projecting. Tabitha walked over and climbed into her Sport Moonbeam. She really enjoyed this hover over all the other ones she had owned. Pride flooded her as she thought of how well it glided over any terrain. *Too bad the law stated one was supposed to stay on existing roadways—stupid rules are made to be broken....* Well, she broke the rules once in awhile. Today, though, she headed back to the city—on the roadway.

The computer in her hover announced that she had an incoming phone call. When Tabitha pushed the receiver button, a man's face of about twenty-eight years appeared in three-dimensional form on the dash of the vehicle.

"Hello," spoke the image before her. "We need to talk."

"Mark," Tabitha replied. "I really don't want to talk. We've been through everything already. Let's just face the facts. You got me pregnant, you want me to get an abortion, and I'm going to do it. You won't have to put up with your child—*No*, Tabitha thought, *don't think of the fetus as a child*—getting in the way."

After a pause, she added, "Mark, I know some time has passed since the start of all this, but I still don't want to live with you. I thought at one time I would want to try, but I don't. All your freedom is gone when you are confined to one relationship. I know you said I would be free to see other men, but you would still have partial control over my life, and I don't want that!"

"Tabitha, I love you," Mark said, desperately trying to control his emotions.

"I hate you," Tabitha responded. "I want you to know that I don't want to marry you, and I never did." Tabitha wondered why it was so easy for her to lie. She just did not want a family keeping her from enjoying life. Grandma had said not to get trapped by other people. She would have strongly supported Tabitha's desire to stay free of long-lasting commitments, as well as her decision to get the abortion. Where was she when Tabitha needed her?!

Mark seemed stunned. "No, Tabitha, you're lying. I don't believe you. You do love me. Besides, we don't have to get married—most people don't anymore. We can just live together—with no strings attached!"

"Good-by, Mark. Like I said earlier, we have nothing to talk about. I intend to have the abortion done today so I can think about other things! When I'm done with this business, there will be nothing left of you in my life!"

As she started to disconnect the call, she saw the hurt overwhelm Mark's face. Tabitha pushed the disconnect button as she heard Mark's weakened voice reply, "I don't care about the child, Tabitha. I just want you!"

8:20 a.m.

Maria kept her assault weapon ready as she watched the huge hover transport float up to the docking bay on a cushion of air about three feet thick. With expert precision, it backed carefully into the narrow opening.

Paul opened the vehicle's rear trailer doors with the help of another man. Besides Maria, there were several other men and women scattered around the scene. All were armed, poised and ready as if expecting trouble momentarily. A few seconds later, a very large group of small children were carefully but urgently hurried in through the open doors of the hover transport's trailer.

A dozen or so elderly people walked along with the children. Some of the older ones needed help to walk, but the stronger ones helped keep them and the children moving. Several of the armed men and women joined them inside as Paul closed the large doors behind them.

Paul walked over next to Maria and put his arm around her as the hover's power plant began to increase its roar, and the huge vehicle pulled away.

"There goes another bunch of 'em," he said. He stretched his neck and shoulders as if relieving them of the burden that they bore. "Number Seven will be here soon with the plans. Then we will go and get another collection to raise."

Maria pressed close to Paul as she felt the emptiness swell around her. She knew she would miss the children terribly—especially Blessed and his cute smile. She knew she was being selfish. She wanted them with her, but there was too much danger of them falling into the hands of the government here. The risk was too great.

Their job had been simple. The order was always simple. Rescue them from abortion—even in the very process of the execution. *Get 'em big enough to travel, then say good-by,* she thought sadly. Maria felt a part of her leave with each group.

She spoke softly as she leaned her head onto Paul's chest, "God save the children."

9:15 a.m.

Number Seven leaned against the desk behind him, half-sitting on it. Around about him stood eight men and women, most of them in their twenties. *Why is it always the young who must give their lives for what is right?* he thought. *Maybe it's because they have the courage and the foolishness to do it. We older and wiser people find reasons not to die.* Number Seven sadly realized that he had dealt with the issue of life and death for so long that it had come to seem almost natural, and that concerned him.

Everything he did made him concerned. The undercover work, the purposeful deceptions that surrounded his existence—all were for the right reasons, but the pathway was difficult to justify for a believer. Would he be praised or condemned for his actions when he stood before the Almighty? An old saying came to his mind, *It is never wrong to do right; it is never right to do wrong.* God was the only consistency in Number Seven's life, the only relationship that had ever worked. *God grant me wisdom!* he prayed silently again. How many times a day, even in the last hour, had he breathed that desperate prayer?

"Well, there you have it," Number Seven continued verbally. "Are there any questions?" As he measured their response to his fifteen-minute rescue mission briefing, he looked them over and was very proud. These young people had faced death once today already in an SBI raid and had managed to escape with all of the children and elderly people. He deeply respected their feelings and instincts, and listened carefully when they spoke.

"You are certain that our contact inside is alive and well?" Paul asked. "I don't fancy the idea of walking into a trap."

Number Seven stood up. He spoke in a rather serious tone. "I'll put it to you this way, Paul. He was alive and well this morning when I talked to him. You know the risks. There is a leak somewhere in our organization. We haven't been able to find where. SBI is very serious about stopping us." The older man shrugged his shoulders. "What can I say? You may very well die today."

"We understand," Paul replied. "We know there are no guarantees. We go for the children."

Number Seven nodded in agreement. "I know." Looking in each face, he stopped at Maria's. He could not bring himself to tell her what had happened to her brother's body. It really was not necessary for her to know.

"Maria," he said.

"Yes?"

Number Seven paused before speaking. "This is the first time you will be going in to rescue a Class II abortion. Do you think you can handle it?"

Maria took a deep breath and said, "I think so. I want to do this for my brother."

Number Seven nodded. "It is a holy war," he said. "It is time we ask help from our best ally."

There, in that small dingy room on the outer edges of a lonely death-filled city, nine people bowed in prayer. "Deliver us from evil. God save the children."

Chapter Eight

9:40 a.m.

Tabitha's mother sat in her comfortable recliner browsing casually through a three-dimensional photo album of her family history. Even though old age had definitely set in, Martha was considered very beautiful among her friends and that gave her immense satisfaction.

Her family history was one of independence for women and that too made her proud. The elderly lady smiled. The right to choose was basic in her mind for a woman's happiness. Unfortunately, the logical conclusion and result of her philosophy was causing her great problems in her current situation.

With a deep sigh, Martha touched another control and a 3D image of a youthful appearing man appeared in front of her. Handsome young Scott Harrison, Martha thought with a smile in her heart. She sure had made the wrong choice when it came to him. She should never have had that abortion. He was so against it.

Martha quickly touched another control and the image of her grandmother, Tasha Jones, appeared before her as a young mother. Martha smiled at the baby in her arms. That was Martha's mother, Valerie. She had been a very pretty baby, but she was such a fierce woman when she grew up! A lot of Valerie was in Martha's daughter, Tabitha. Tabitha had such a temper!

The old woman turned off the photo album. Enough of family genealogy. She had to admit that the possibilities of reincarnation excited her very much. She wanted to understand her past so that she might advance to the future. At this moment, however, she was interested in the present. She turned on the 3D unit to watch the news.

The front door opened and Martha stood up as Tabitha entered the living room. The three-dimensional projection of the newswoman on the television platform reported that a possible cure for the killer H.S.-23 virus was undergoing testing and might be available for general use as soon as next spring. The older woman touched a control on the sofa and the newswoman disappeared. The room was silent.

"Well, Tabitha," her mother inquired in a brisk manner, "what have you decided?"

"Mother," Tabitha responded, "I've made up my mind. I'm going to the abortion clinic today."

Martha softened some in her tone and replied, "I'm not really sure that I want you to do this. I've grown use to the idea of having the child to do things with in my reclining years."

"Mother, that's pretty selfish of you. It's my life, my fetus, my problem, and what difference is it to you?!

Since when did you become moral! You were quite satisfied to watch Grandma die and get her money. I just want to take this—thing—out of my life!" Losing control, she cursed and swore at her mother and her undesired offspring.

Tabitha's mother stepped back. "Don't talk about your child like that!" she cried, her voice cracking at a near scream. She had not meant to react so out of control, but now it was too late. The room filled with immediate tension and anger. One did not make Tabitha angry unless one was ready for a long drawn-out fight. She never backed down.

"Child?!" Tabitha screamed back. "It's not a child. It's proven not to be human until it is past the sixth cycle! Why don't you leave me alone!"

Her mother reached out to her, but Tabitha pulled away and stepped back herself. "Just leave me alone!"

"Tabitha," her mother spoke softly, "give yourself time to deal with this without making a rash decision you can never undo."

"Oh, Mother," she said and shook her head. "You don't understand. You better watch how you talk to me, or I'll take you to a Reanimation Center so fast you'll be dead before you can argue."

Her mother looked away. She was quiet for a moment before she replied. "I just don't want you to do this thing. How could you have allowed yourself to get into such a mess? Why didn't you stop the pregnancy in the early stages before we got to this point? It's just that it is so hard to do it now!"

Tabitha felt frustration rising inside her. She answered, "I was going to, Mother. I wish to God that I had, but I didn't, and now I want to put it behind me."

Her mother turned to her. She was silent for a moment, then spoke. "I think I was wrong to let my mother teach you the laws of life. I didn't think you would become so hardened."

"What did you expect, Mother?" Tabitha asked in a sharp tone. "I am my grandmother. She may well have chosen to walk beside me for now instead of going on. I feel her presence near me all the time. Did you know that she talks to me at night when everyone is asleep?"

"No." Her mother suddenly looked very frightened. "Be careful of my mother, Tabitha. She was powerful while she lived on this earth—she must be powerful on the higher plane too. She may even possess you!"

Tabitha's eyes grew wilder. She drew herself up and spoke in her grandmother's voice, "I already possess her!"

Tabitha's mother screamed. "Get out of here!" she shouted.

Tabitha shook her head and almost lost her balance. Her mother reached out and steadied her daughter.

"Why did you shout at me, Mother?" Tabitha asked.

"You don't know?" Martha asked.

"No," Tabitha answered.

Frightened, her will to fight broken, the older woman gave in. "Maybe you are right. If you feel this is the answer, then I won't stop you." Feeling weak and frail, she sat down on the sofa, leaned her head against a cushion, and closed her eyes. *Demon-possessed people. That is what the preacher in prison had said on the television interview. Was it possible? or was it really her mother controlling Tabitha?* The older woman felt near death—now she wanted to die.

Emptiness filled Tabitha as she walked toward a near-by bedroom door. She paused and faced her mother who was still seated with her eyes closed.

"Mother?"

"Yes, Tabitha?"

"What will my father think?"

There was a long pause before the older woman answered. She finally turned and looked at her daughter, "I don't think you should tell him. He was looking forward to spending his last year with his grandchild. This will break his heart. Anyway, I was thinking about having him put to rest early because he is in so much pain. Now, I'll just plan on it. I really don't think he'll mind."

Tabitha felt somewhat relieved with the news. She loved her father, but he was so unreasonable at times. *Old age is such a terrible thing—it robs the mind of the ability to think straight.* "Whatever you think is best, Mother," she said as she left the room.

Her mother watched as she departed. The older woman sighed and thought to herself, *I suppose I'll be next.*

10:05 a.m.

Scott Harrison sat quietly in his office looking over a small mountain of legal documents he had just requested from his computer. He felt tired, and there was no question that his heart wasn't in his work. Harrison, already well past the mandatory age of termination, was the oldest and most respected member of the SBI organization. He found himself wishing to be any place other than where he currently was at the moment. *Time passes so slowly,* he thought as he checked his watch again.

Scott leaned back in his chair. With no desire to do the work in front of him, he found himself reminiscing about the past. Scenes from the last century began to pass through his memory.

The elderly man found himself relaxing as the face of a very pretty girl took full blossom in his thoughts. He had forgotten how beautiful she had been. He wondered where she was. He felt certain that she was still in the city. How strange it was to live near her for so many years and not know where she was. He could have found out easily enough with his top-level access to the SBI files, but there had never been a desire to make the four or five commands it would have taken.

There was also bitterness in his heart toward this woman of his memory. Not an active boiling bitterness, but a tamed, calm sadness—more like a deep disappointment than actual bitterness. Scott sat there wandering why God had never taken it from his heart.

He had never married, and in a very real sense, he felt robbed of a home and family. He should have been planning a pleasant weekend with his wife and boy instead of passing another lonely weekend in his high-rise.

Strange, he always thought of the unborn child as a boy. He really had no knowledge of what it had been. It really did not matter. After all of his father's mind games and the DNA laser-manipulation of his formative years, Scott had made a promise to himself that he would never use his offspring for his own advantage.

He found himself mentally relaxing again only now realizing that he actually had tensed his whole body. He sighed inwardly, and within his mind, he began talking with this lost woman of his past...

Martha, why did you kill our innocent unborn son? There were other choices. I still hate you, and I still love you. The abortion changed my life and set me on a course that has led me here to this office. I wish you could have seen the things I've seen."

Yes, there was some bitterness deep inside. He felt it now at that memory. *Let the anger go up toward God*, he thought. *It'll kill you if it stays inside.*

On an impulse, for the first time Scott entered the five commands needed to find the woman of his past. With a final entry, the 3-D call was placed.

Tabitha's mother heard the house computer announce an incoming call. She acknowledged it, but no one appeared on the viewer stage.

Scott watched her confused face on his viewer stage. *She is beautiful in her old age*, he thought. *She must be near termination.* He felt sorry for her. Then he pushed the disconnect control. No time for that.

Scott's mind drifted from his lost love to his father in a strange sort of transaction. He concluded that some of the hate he was feeling at the moment probably was directed at his dad.

His father had been a terribly self-centered person, the kind of guy television villains—and modern heroes—were made of. Scott shook his head and half-smiled. His father, the great Karl Harrison, had been shot and killed by an old man who caught on to one of his swindle operations back in '73. Scott was in his early twenties at the time. He didn't miss his dad much.

Relationships! Most of Scott's relationships had been failures. Martha, his father, all the others—the psychologist had warned him that his relationship with his father would have a tendency to ruin all relationships. Scott knew the insecurity of not knowing his mother and not trusting his father. It was not until middle age that he'd found a relationship, a truth, that stayed always consistent. That was when Scott, a rising star at SBI, had secretly found a Bible in the SBI's mammoth property room for confiscated contraband. That book had had mind-bending results. No one else at the SBI Headquarters knew of his Bible study, and he was not about to tell them—it could mean instant demotion, imprisonment, and even death.

He broke suddenly from his thoughts at the realization that a woman stood directly in front of him—and not just any woman—it was the notorious Rachel Morgan, herself. "Hello, Rachel," he responded. "Nice of you to have slithered in."

"You're all too kind, Scotty," she replied. "Your door was open so I made myself welcome. I knew you wouldn't mind."

Scott's eye brows raised. "Clairvoyant, huh?" With a wave of his hand, he gestured to her to have a seat. She nodded a thank you and sat down. Leaning forward in his seat, he asked, "Why have you graced me with your presence? I'm sure you have many Code Three violators to arrest. Why have you taken time out of your busy schedule?"

Rachel leaned back, stretched out her legs, crossed them, and let her face smile a very charming smile of victory. "We know there is going to be a raid on the Clinic today." There was excitement in her voice, although she concealed it for the most part.

Scott covered his shocked reaction to her statement very well. His only outward response was, "I suppose you have come here to gloat that you discovered this before me?"

Her smile deepened. "Yes, I did as a matter of fact. How does it feel to be upstaged by one of your juniors?"

There was no comment in Scott's mind at the moment that satisfied him so he just said, "Congratulations, Rachel. You have done an impressive job for as long as I have known you. I suppose you have everything covered. Care to let me in on the details?" With a casual movement of his eyes, Scott noted the time on the computer screen.

Rachel leaned her head at an angle, causing her hair to move forward, partially covering one of her eyes. It was a deliberate move to reflect a sense of mystery. "Details?" Rachel replied. "Share them? No, I really don't think so. This one is all mine. I don't want you stealing part of the credit. We know Number Seven is here in the city, and we know that he's working inside this very building!"

"Come on!" Scott laughed. "He's not that stupid. We have his body rhythms measured. We would pick him up right away with the scanners."

"No, I don't think so," was her response. Rachel stood up and walked over to the window to look down on the people in the city below. "His organization has developed a distorter that masks his body signals. We wouldn't even know he was here. Besides, I'm not so sure we have the right readings on him anyway!"

Scott got up and walked over next to her. "The readings are right. I got them myself."

"I know," Rachel answered. "Scott, do you ever feel any personal disgust at our job? It's sort of like being a tax collector, isn't it?"

"Rachel, my dear," Scott replied with a smile, "do you think I'm stupid enough to say or imply anything against SBI? You probably have some tiny voice monitor under that flattering little jacket of yours ready to record any words of treason that I might utter."

Rachel smiled, reached into her jacket, and pulled out a very small tape recorder. She shut it off. "You're not much fun anymore, Scotty," she said. She set the tape recorder down and faced the older man. "How do you really feel? No tricks this time. It's just you and me here, alone." She reached up and wrapped both arms seductively around his neck and stepped toward him.

"Nervous," Scott answered and stepped back. He walked over to his desk and sat down. "But, I will tell you how I really feel. I believe that one day the resistance is going to win in this nation. I believe there is a price to pay for our deeds and actions. I only hope it will not happen in my lifetime. I would hate to face that responsibility. Don't worry about quoting me. I've already shared those words with SBI's High Command. They fear it too—that's why they're pushing so hard. You know what else I think?"

Rachel half-grinned and replied, "I wouldn't miss it."

Scott stood up, leaned forward, rested the finger tips of his hands on the top of his desk, and said, "I believe you're afraid it's true, too! That is why you're the best at what you do. You're afraid this big monster will turn on you, and you'll be branded like some twentieth century war criminal in a future school history book. It's all kind of funny, you know. We all lie to ourselves. It makes it easier to deal with life."

Rachel Morgan stood very quietly in front of Scott for almost a minute. Then she spoke. "You really are no fun anymore, Scotty. Where do you think our mistake has been?"

"I'll tell you where, Rachel," Scott lifted the level of his voice just slightly. "When we concluded that we had the knowledge to determine what was right or wrong. We have become gods in human bodies."

"OK, Scott, so we've become gods," Rachel responded. "So what. You don't really believe there is a real God, do you? That we are going to have to stand before some all-powerful being and explain our way out of this? Come off it, Scott. What is really bugging you?"

Scott looked Rachel straight in the eyes. "What if we're wrong? What if the fetus really is human—like us?"

Rachel dropped her eyes just slightly so she did not have to look directly at his eyes. "Scott," she said, "let it go."

Scott persisted. "What if the fetus really is human?"

Her reply was mechanical. "The fetus has been scientifically proven subhuman until after the sixth cycle."

Scott's response was harsh. "That's a bunch of rot, and you know it! What if the fetus is human?"

Rachel's surrender amazed Scott. "You already know the real answer to your question."

"You're right," he said. "I just want to hear you say it."

Rachel took a deep breath. "All right," she replied. "The fetus is human. We all know that. There is no difference in human existence whether it's the sixth, seventh, or whatever cycle. It makes no difference though, Scott, and you know it. We as a society have decided that it is the sixth cycle, and that is enough to make it the sixth cycle."

Scott turned his back on Rachel. He spoke softly with bowed head. "Don't you have nightmares?"

"Why? Should I?"

Scott was silent for a moment. When he spoke, there was a hint of anger in his voice, although it was clear that he was trying to maintain his control. "The fetus," he began speaking softly. He paused a moment. "Some of the fetuses scream when they are aborted."

Rachel felt a chill go up her spine. She found herself becoming angry. She fired back, "I personally liked the

Injection method because I felt it was much more humane. It was not as cost effective as the new Incision method is..." Rachel stopped in the middle of her statement. Why was she defending her actions? Then a terrible thought hit her. She was being baited by Scott. Maybe he was trying to set her up.

The old Hermit, she thought. *You don't do what he has done in life without being smart.* She had thought she had him, and all along he was playing games with her. She smiled at him. She would have the last laugh.

"Nice try, Scotty," Rachel said. "I'll see you later after my big catch." She paused at the door and turned. She spoke with a tone of real victory. "We've located Emergency Shelter Twelve, and all their main leaders are stationed there! There will be a raid—she looked down at her watch—in about twelve minutes. Wish us luck!"

Scott waved good-by as she walked out. He took one last glance at the computer—10:38 a.m. There was not much time.

Chapter Nine

11:02 a.m.

Mark pulled his hovermobile to a stop about a block from the abortion clinic. Shutting the motor off, he half-slid down into his seat and waited. As for a plan, he really did not have any. Somehow, he had to own Tabitha, and that was all that was important. As Mark sat there, he thought through what a mistake it had been to put himself in the position of coming to love Tabitha. She was so beautiful, but she was so selfish. He was selfish too, but somehow that was different.

Almost with a start, Mark realized that Tabitha had driven past him on her way to the clinic. He sat up and started his vehicle all in one motion. Pulling into traffic, he managed to stay fairly close to her. Maybe there was a chance, he thought. The ancients certainly brought her by him.

Tabitha's vehicle pulled into a parallel parking place in front of the abortion clinic. Mark was able to park about four spaces down from her. He was fairly certain that she had not seen him yet. He immediately jumped from his hover and ran toward Tabitha as she started climbing out from her driver's seat. It never occurred to Mark that his actions were drawing the attention of SBI security guards who were monitoring the perimeter of the outer clinic grounds.

George Keller, head of the Reanimation Center's Security Force, watched the scene on television monitors. In his late forties, he was considered ruthless by those who worked with him. They had judged him right, and he knew it. One could not have any weakness and do his job. This world would eat you alive! He dispatched two patrols to deal with the situation. *No one harassed anybody that wanted to come into a Reanimation Center for an abortion. Not while he was on duty.*

Outside on the street, Tabitha froze in place next to her vehicle as Mark ran up. He stopped within a couple feet of her, and reaching out to her said, "I had to come. I really don't care what you do with this child. I want you. I know you don't want to marry me, but let's work it out. Let's solve it. I know we can. Please, Tabitha?"

"Oh, Mark," she said, choking back a sob. "Why did you have to come here? This is hard enough without you trying to complicate it. I don't love you anymore. I don't want you, and I don't want this child! I don't want anything left of you in my life. Now go away and leave me alone!"

"I don't want the child either. It's nothing! Kill it! Keep it! I don't care! I can't live without you!" Mark insisted as he reached for her arm. She jerked it away and pushed at him. He grabbed her hands trying to control her.

"Let go of me!" she screamed. "Get away from me! I hate you!"

"Tabitha, I love you! Please don't!" he pleaded. She pushed hard against him, forcing him off balance. Mark held on, trying to regain that balance. He heard another vehicle pull up beside them, and out of the corner of his eye he saw armed security guards moving toward him. Letting go of Tabitha, he turned to explain to the men coming at him. They did not give him any opportunity. Instead, the first guard punched Mark in the stomach with a night stick. Mark doubled over in pain only to feel more agony as the guard hit him on the back of his head.

"Stop! What are you doing?!" Tabitha shouted at the policemen. "He wasn't hurting me. Please, stop!"

The officers drug Mark into the back of the patrol vehicle. One of them turned to Tabitha reassuringly. He spoke gently. "It's all right, ma'am. We just don't want him disturbing you anymore. This is America. People don't have the right to harass other people."

Tabitha started relaxing. "You won't hurt him anymore, will you?"

"No, I promise you he will be OK," the officer said and left. Tabitha watched the officer leave, then turned and reached into her vehicle. It was time to get it done and over with.

11:15 a.m.

Number Seven walked casually down the street toward a convenience mall. Stepping inside, he walked over to a video phone. Slipping a credit card into a specially designed slot, he waited for the party on the other end to answer. He did not turn on the video part of the phone. A voice spoke from the speaker in the machine, "Alex's Accounting Service. How may I help you?"

Number Seven responded, "Wisdom is better than weapons of war."

The voice on the other end replied, "But one sinner destroyeth much good."

"Urgent message," Number Seven said. "Abort mission. Repeat: abort."

"We can't," came the response. "Two are enroute. They should be pulling up to their destination now. No way to warn them. Truck being monitored on approach. They'll track us and we'll lose Gamma location."

Number Seven felt anger. *I'm too late*, he thought. "Call them anyway. Pull everyone out. Close Gamma location. Put a code Z into effect. Have they raided Emergency Shelter Twelve yet?"

"I don't think so. We've not received any messages!"

"Don't take any chances. Notify them immediately to disappear! SBI has good people on this, and they'll nail us if we don't clear out. Now do it!"

"Yes, sir." The speaker on the phone system went silent. Number Seven sighed a deep breath. Years of work would have to be reversed now. Still, there was no choice. Too many lives were at risk. Hurt filled him as he thought of the children. Thousands would die in abortion clinics before they would be able to start operations again. It was sickening to think that his pro-life organization was filled with betrayal, but until they could weed out the traitors, no one was safe anymore.

Number Seven turned to leave when he realized that Rachel Morgan was standing in the doorway of the mall. A casual glance over his shoulder revealed more SBI agents behind him. It was over.

Rachel smiled in her victory. Even as she did so, Number Seven punched a three digit code into his phone card. Almost instantly, Rachel realized what he was doing. "Stop him!" she screamed. "He's dissolving his phone card!"—but it was too late. The card melted into oblivion. Number Seven smiled at Rachel. The other agents took him by the arms and handcuffs were on his wrists within moments.

Rachel walked forward to within a couple feet of her handcuffed colleague. She spoke with a note of frustration, "Well, Scott, I mean Number Seven, I suppose that was a scramble card, huh?"

"Most likely," Scott Harrison answered. "Too bad that it didn't hold up. It will sure be difficult to trace that call now. I would say almost impossible."

Rachel turned to one of the other agents. "Check it out anyway!" she said. Turning back to Scott, she put her arm around him. "I've felt for years you were Number Seven, but only in my nightmares. I was hoping that I was wrong. I guess I miscalculated."

Scott smiled. "It does seem so," he said.

Rachel sighed. "You know there will be no trial. I will never see you again. You will have to excuse me, though. I have some pressing business. Good-by." She turned and left without waiting for him to answer. It did not matter. Scott knew that there were no replies to be said. He felt tired anyway. There was a sense of sadness about him as the SBI agents led him to their hovercraft. *I'm confident that God will find other soldiers*, he thought as they pulled away.

11:20 a.m.

Paul and Maria backed the hover transport up the clinic docking bay. They had barely stepped out and walked up to the receiving counter when a call came through their radio, but they were too far away to hear it.

Paul spoke to the woman sitting behind the counter. "We're here to pick up a shipment of fetuses. Here is our paper work. Can we do this as quickly as possible?" He threw a clipboard down on the counter. The woman glanced at it.

"You're a day early, but I don't think that will be a problem. There were considerably more abortions this week, so it's good you're here. In fact, I bet that's why they sent you early."

"Yes, we received a call," Maria said.

The woman got up and walked over to a hallway. "Follow me, please. I don't recognize either of you so I don't suppose you know your way around. I'll show you."

"No, this is my first time at this clinic," Paul said honestly. However, he had the whole floor plan memorized. Paul fell in step down the hallway with Maria behind him. They were led into another room. As soon as they stepped in, the door closed behind them. They turned to see themselves surrounded by SBI Security Guards. George Keller, the tallest among them, walked over and searched them. He removed their hand guns and glared at them.

"Take them to C-12," he ordered. Paul and Maria shared a glance for a moment. *Maria is frightened*, Paul thought, *and with good reason. We won't live out the day.*

Chapter Ten

11:30 a.m.

The SBI vehicle pulled up to the processing plant, and three guards led Scott into a back door and down a long hallway. They stopped at another door and one of the guards placed his hand on the entrance square. The door slid open and they stepped inside. The room was filled with human bodies stacked neatly on shelves. *Well, this is the time to be brave,* Scott thought.

"Number Seven," one of the guards called to get his attention. "Any particular shelf you would like to occupy?"

Scott shook his head. "I'm not the fussy type. Which one would you suggest? Actually, that one over there would fit you."

"Funny," the guard replied. "Let's get this over with." The guard and one of his companions started moving toward Scott when the third guard who was behind them spoke.

"Gentlemen," he said, "I hate to spoil this, but don't make any sudden moves." The two guards turned to discover that the third guard had his weapon leveled at them and not their prisoner.

"What?!" the first guard stammered.

The third guard smiled. "The word is not 'what' but good night." He walked over and took a gas hose from off the wall. Signaling the men to come over next to him, he placed it under their noses. In a few moments they collapsed. "That ought to hold them for a couple of hours."

Scott walked up to the remaining guard who stood over his companions and said, "Jimmy, you sure took your time."

"Sorry."

"Well, let's not waste anymore," Number Seven responded. "We have a vehicle to intercept and some people to rescue."

"I understand that Canada is nice this time of year," Jimmy remarked as he led Scott from the room.

"Yes, it is," the older man casually commented. "I've been planning to take a vacation for years."

11:45 a.m.

Rachel Morgan walked into the clinic's containment room next to the processing plant. The machines were at a full roar. She felt a personal satisfaction that she had purchased more stock in Recycling Incorporated. Her dividend check would surely be one of the best she had received.

In front of her sat three people handcuffed to their individual chairs. The person on her left was a girl in her twenties. *Pretty*, Rachel thought. The other two did not catch her attention.

"Well?" she asked the SBI agents that surrounded the prisoners.

"Nothing so far," George Keller replied. "The man on the right is not one of them. At least, I don't think so. He was harassing a young lady outside who came here for an abortion. The other two are definitely part of Number Seven's team."

Rachel Morgan walked over to a very frightened Mark who looked up at her. He appeared to be badly beaten. She reached over and pulled a laser revolver from one of the guards holsters, and in one movement, placed the pistol to the startled man's forehead and pulled the trigger. A beam of light shot from the weapon, striking his head and causing his body to jerk backward with the impact. Blood instantly poured from the wound as his body went limp.

Maria fought the sobs that swelled inside her. Paul made a jerking motion against his chair as if to rise when another guard backhanded him down into his chair. "Why did you shoot him?" Paul asked. "He wasn't one of us."

Rachel smiled at him. Her answer was simple. "I wanted you to know that I have total power over your lives, and that I mean to find out all that I want to know. I want you to know that even God cannot deliver you now."

Paul spoke softly and with determination. "Yes, He can, if He wants." Rachel slapped Paul's face with the barrel of the pistol.

"Total power over your lives," she repeated. "I have the laws of our country behind me. You have nothing."

Maria answered this time, fully aware of the blood draining from Paul's cut face. "You only have our bodies. You don't have us."

Rachel laughed. "Dear Miss Innocent, the things that I could do to your bodies would give you nightmares. Tell me what I want to know. Tell me now!" She pointed the pistol directly at Maria's face.

"No, I won't," Maria said. She closed her eyes and waited. She heard the pistol go off beside her. Jerking her head sideways, she saw Paul slumped over. Maria screamed in agony.

12:30 p.m.

Rachel walked into the Termination Room of the clinic. She was followed by several SBI agents and a very despondent Maria.

"Set her down over there where she will have a clear view," Rachel ordered. After the men led her to a chair near the termination area, Rachel walked over to her, leaned close to her ear and began to speak soothingly. "Give it up. I can spare your life. Why die for those men when they deserted you and let you walk into this trap?"

When there was no response from Maria of any kind, Rachel seemed a little annoyed. She spoke again. "We have captured Number Seven. We already have all the information we need from him," she lied. Maria looked up, but she did not speak.

Rachel sighed, and made a mock gesture of defeat. "Send in the next patient who is scheduled for an abortion," she told an elderly nurse who was standing by the door. Rachel turned to Maria and smiled. "I have decided to give you a ringside seat for the rest of the day's performance. If you decide to talk, let me know, and we'll cut the show short!"

"What do we have coming in?" a doctor asked as he scrubbed his hands.

"A female fetus of the fourth cycle," replied an efficient young nurse.

"Has it been checked for infections?" the doctor inquired casually.

"Yes, the blood work was completed ten minutes ago. Nothing irregular." The nurse took her position next to the table. She added, "There is no reason why we cannot do the incision method."

"Good." The doctor said as he picked up his favorite scalpel, an antique 1997 model made from rare virgin surgical steel. He'd almost built his entire practice with this fine medical tool.

Maria started whining. Terrible fear and sorrow overwhelmed her. She had never witnessed an actual abortion of the Class II level before, but she knew what was coming.

"Please," she said. "Don't."

"Quit whimpering," Rachel ordered.

The door opened. The elderly nurse entered the room leading a frightened little four-year-old girl by the hand.

A woman in her twenties followed. The efficient young nurse walked over to the woman and held out her clipboard for her signature.

"I don't know," the woman said in a hesitant manner.

"It's all right," the young nurse replied. "You're doing the right thing. Everyone gets a little shaky at this point—especially the first time. Just sign the release and you will be able to leave. Go ahead."

Tabitha reached down for the clipboard and pen. Almost in a daze, she wrote her name. The elderly nurse put her arms around the shaken mother and began to escort her from the room.

"Where are you going, Mommy?" the little girl asked. The child started to sob. "Don't leave me here by myself!"

"Come with me, dear," the elderly nurse said as she led Tabitha through the door. "It will be all right. Don't pay attention. We have everything under control." The nurse pulled the door closed behind her.

The little girl ran toward the door, but the younger nurse caught her and picked her up. "Don't be afraid," she said to the child. "It will be all right. We have a kind doctor here that loves children." The child felt secure in the nurse's arms and started relaxing. The nurse brought her over and laid her down on the operating table.

Maria broke into total panic. She started to jump up and shout a warning when one of the SBI agents pulled her down to the chair again, holding a hand tightly on her mouth.

138

"Shame on you," Rachel scolded. "You'll frighten the child needlessly."

The little girl did become frightened and started to squirm. The nurse held her tight. The doctor reached down with the scalpel and began to cut the child's throat. The little girl only screamed partially before gagging.

12:45 p.m.

A lonely, despairing Maria was led from the abortion clinic's rear doors to a waiting SBI patrol vehicle resting by the curb. There were only two guards with her and none of them had their arms handcuffed to her, revealing their total confidence in their victory.

They opened the rear door of the hovercraft and forcibly set her inside. Then they slammed the door shut and signed over the prisoner to the driver and another elderly man who sat in the front seat. As the vehicle moved away from the curb, Maria noticed that the protective cage divider between the front and back seat was lowering. In shock, she watched as Number Seven turned around and spoke to her.

"Sorry to have rescued you in such an undramatic manner," he said, "but I'm getting too old for the action sequences."

Maria let out a sigh of relief. Then sadness overwhelmed her again. Looking straight at Scott, she shared, "Paul and another man are dead. That woman, Rachel Morgan, just shot them both."

The older man nodded his head. He spoke in sympathetic tones. "We know. We saw SBI guards carry them to the processing plant. Don't worry about Rachel Morgan. We've arranged to make this escape look like she planned it. She will have to do a lot of explaining—if they give her a chance."

"What do we do now?" Maria asked.

"We will head up to Canada," Number Seven replied. "We have to go into seclusion for awhile until we can rebuild. I fear in my heart they may have given us a death blow. However, I understand that there may be actual war between Canada and the United States. A storm is forming on the horizon of human history. The judgement may be coming. God grant Canada the ability to crush this ungodly nation."

Maria settled back in her seat and watched the people of the city through the glass window as the vehicle moved along. *None of them out there understand what is happening or really even care*, she thought. She noticed a couple walking side by side, holding hands. Despair and sadness overwhelmed her. Tears began to slide down her cheeks. *I miss you, Paul*, she spoke inwardly.

Maria's sadness deepened and she shut out the rest of the universe—except for one tiny four-year-old child etched in clear vision in her mind's eye. *I will never forget you, little girl*, Maria promised. *I will never forget you, and I will never give up. I keep my promises.*

Epilogue

Europe

Year 2127
(17 years after the Canadian Conflict)

7:35 a.m.

Terra set on her bed with her legs curled up to her chin and her arms wrapped around her knees. She watched the light of the room increase slowly as daylight became a part of the morning. The sunlight gave her welcomed warmth as the rays pushed the darkened portion of the room from her. Her soul felt restless. Terra's morning was already a long one—she had been up since about 5:00 a.m.. She was weary from study but felt very confident that she was well prepared. She had reviewed so many facts that there were moments that it seemed her head would pound itself off of her body.

This was a very special day. It was her eighteenth birthday. It was also the day of her second right of passage. She had passed the first one with high merit when she was twelve years old. Her parents had been very proud of her. They had taken her shopping in Asia for the evening. Terra felt she would make them proud of her again.

Terra loved her parents. They loved her too. She was their pride and joy. They had often shared with her that of all they possessed, she was their most valuable asset. Terra knew she was special because she had been selected from among all the others as "quality life with promise."

She was all a couple could ever want in an offspring. Terra was aware of her slim and trim figure and her beautiful eyes. She smiled. Then, there was her charm. She could talk her dad into anything. Her mom, though. Her mom was everything she wanted to be.

Terra threw herself backward on the bed and stared up at the ceiling. She thought of her mother with pride and pleasure. Mother had joined up with Father twenty years before and had moved to Europe from America just before the Canadian Conflict had broken out. The end result was a new America where the laws were changing rapidly. The freedom to choose was being lost with each passing year. Her parents had been very lucky to leave when they had. Terra's mother called it wisdom from the ancients.

Terra was an only child, at least in the modern sense of the term. Her parents had deposited the material necessary to make five fetuses at the German Institute for Human Development.

The capsules containing the zygotes had undergone preliminary genetic testing resulting in one fetus being rejected before it reached self-sustained existence. It had been disposed of through the usual processing plants. Two others had failed at the two year cycle of existence because of behavioral and emotional development. They were of the right age to use for special scientific experimentation.

Terra shuddered once again feeling very thankful that that had not been her fate.

One other, besides herself, had shown real promise. She would have qualified for early human status at the sixth year cycle if her parents had wanted two children. However, her parents had wanted only one. One child to pour out their love on; they had selected Terra.

Terra was glad she had survived the years of analyzation and had been presented to her parents on her sixth birthday with the state's approval. Sometimes the other one that had almost made it haunted her mind. Terra had seen her only once, but she well remembered her smiling happy face and friendly wave. Terra wondered what had happened to her.

Now Terra was eighteen and ready for the freedom and pleasures of Adulthood. All she had to do was pass one more test and she would graduate with excellent educational and career opportunities. *Well, no better time than the present*, she thought.

Walking quietly down the hallway so as not to disturb her parents, she stepped onto the phone stage. What a shock for her parents to wake up and discover her wearing her newly acquired rating patch. Terra wanted to surprise her parents very much. She would take the test before they got up.

Sitting down at the control panel, she told the computer she was ready. Terra could feel the adrenalin pumping through her system. She was hyped and knew it. The thrill was exciting. The first questions were easy enough, and Terra breezed through them. This was going better than she thought.

Ten minutes passed. The questions were a little more difficult, but she felt she had everything under control. Twenty minutes. *I've got to get done before Mom and Dad get up,* she thought. *I've got to surprise them. Careful though, I've got to score high.*

Thirty minutes passed. The questions were extremely difficult. Terra was growing nervous. How many had she missed? She wished she knew. *Got to be careful.*

Forty minutes. *This was a very hard question.* Terra wished she had studied that section more completely. She reached forward to push her selected answer. *What if I'm wrong? How many have I missed?*

Terra looked at her hand. It was shaking terribly. *Get a hold of yourself, girl. It's just a question. Besides, they say it is painless. You can do it.*

Terra analyzed the question again. Yes, she knew the answer. *Of course.* Reaching forward, she pushed her selected choice. *Oh, God!* she thought as the phone stage lit up. Her parents walked into the family room just in time to see Terra disappear.

"No!" her mother, Tabitha, screamed. With that, Tabitha collapsed into her husband's arms. "Oh, Grandmother! Not Terra," she wept out loud.

Out in space, above the atmosphere, Terra appeared. In total silence, over several agonizing moments, her body exploded from decompression.

When the Son of Man cometh, shall He
find faith on the earth?

Luke 18:8

Author's Personal Note

In the fifteenth century before the birth of Christ, Canaanite parents placed their living infant children on the scorching hot hands of a pagan idol and danced to wild music to drown out the screams of their offspring. These selected human sacrifices held no personal value to their society except to advance the success of their fellow humans by insuring that the gods would be kind to them. History is filled with people and parents who chose themselves over their children—not because they are really any different than the parents of today, but because their instructors of right and wrong, the parents of the parents, decided to live without the values of absolute right from an absolute Lawgiver.

The vulnerable in any society are always at risk first. When children are a commodity, a possession, even if they are a cherished possession, they will be abused. Nor will a society stop with abusing their children. Just as parents come to look upon their children as objects of ownership, so will a society come to look upon its people as owned and belonging to the state. Without accountability to God, there is no reason for the collective whole not to move its rights ahead, over the rights of the one.

Accountability to God is the real issue and the only hope of solving right and wrong. First, there must be a personal relationship with the true God in the person of Jesus Christ. The Lord of Glory Himself said, "No one comes unto the Father, but by Me."

Historically, social change always follows repentance and revival. Then there comes a time to stand and to say "no" to the ever-changing whims of a people and a nation that has decided that personal pleasure and satisfaction take a higher priority than human life. There is a higher law above the laws of men. When we stop basing our human laws on that higher law and the One who gave it, we have opened the door to the desires of humanity, and the powerful of humanity will become the lawgivers. The weak, the old, and the unborn will not give the laws.

You may not agree with this book. You may even conclude that this story cannot happen. At the very least, you may want to ignore its message.

However, like it or not, this book is the final logical conclusion of life under the new lawgivers once they have gained the right to make the laws.

John Thomas Rogers
Springville, Utah
August, 1992